Dragonbound IX

Great Blue Liberator

Rebecca Shelley

 Wonder Realms Books

Cover art © Dusan Kostic | Dreamstime.com
Interior art © Rocich | Dreamstime.com

ISBN-13: 978-0692500521

Published by Wonder Realms Books

To my great-uncle Lt. Charles Ralph Campbell, pilot of a B-24 Liberator, who died heroically when his plane was shot down on a mission to free Europe on December 11, 1944.

From Lt. Campbell's last letter home:

Dear Dad,

There's a little white piece of paper in operations that has my name on it and 35 squares. I'm sort of living right there on that piece of paper. Every time I come back from a mission, no matter how rough it was or how much we got shot up, I feel good when my whole crew is OK and we walk in and see another one of those white squires colored red. Just a few more and we'll be seeing the ones we love at home. Of course, besides just finishing our missions all of us like to feel that we're helping to finish this thing as fast as possible.

Dad, I find the things that occupy my mind most are the plain, ordinary things of life. I want to come home just to live for the joy of living and doing.

I want to get up in the morning, do a good hard day's work, eat a good meal at a good family table, say "hello" to neighbors, shoot pheasants, walk out through a pretty field of spuds, drive to town through the snow, go to church on Sunday with my Dad, wrestle with the boys and tease Mom and the girls, sing in the choir, have a family dinner together on Thanksgiving, go fishing, haul more beans with my truck than the next guy can with his, hug my Mom, marry the sweetest girl in the world, do as fine a job raising a family as my Dad did, build a house and help to make it a home.

A million things like that are what I want to live for, Dad. When I hear a beautiful piece of music that's what it says, and when I pray, those are the things I ask my Heavenly Father to let me do. . . . and I thank him very much for my parents.

Love,

Ralph

The Great North

Mulissat

Theategilag Sound

Kundiland

Maran

Darvat

Eastern Isles

Mendra

Huayna

Wareham

Great Blue Nesting Grounds

Golden Paktes

Temple Ullasoth

Maran Colony

Daro

Varnan Colony

Varna

Stonefountain

Untamed Lands

Edge of the World

Dragonbound

Chapter One

Kanvar sat on Dharanidhar's back on a windswept Darvat beach. Clouds covered the moon, casting the heaving ocean waves in nighttime shadows. Kanvar shivered in the cold wind and squinted across the water as the ships of Bolivar's fleet sailed away and disappeared. His sense of the people on the ships had vanished long before they boarded. No man, woman, or child, once made aware of their cause was allowed to remove their protective iron helmets. To Kanvar's mind, Bolivar's war fleet was unmanned, a ghost fleet sailing toward Varna, driven before the cold gale that whipped the water into monstrous waves. Kanvar stroked the crossbow his grandfather had made him, grateful that Lord Theodoric had been able to summon it from the Kundiland jungle where it had fallen when Khalid had captured Kanvar and taken him to Stonefountain.

1

Dragonbound IX

Dharanidhar growled in complaint and tucked his wings tight against his body. Kanvar shifted in his leather saddle and double-checked that the straps that held him in place were secure.

I agree, Dhar, but what can we do? Kanvar spoke into Dharanidhar's mind. *You and I both know better than to fly in a storm like this.* Both Kanvar and Dharanidhar were still living with the agonizing consequences of the last time they'd tried to fly across this ocean in a storm.

Lord Theodoric and Ishayu have gone with the fleet. Even LaShawn and Damodar are flying tonight. Surely if they don't fear to accompany the fleet, we can go too. Dharanidhar spread his wings, but the wind caught them in a forceful gust, and Dharanidhar had to strain to bring them back to his sides. He growled in annoyance and sank to the sand.

Frost chirped in sympathy and flapped down to land on Dharanidhar's dragonstone. Kivi, who lay against Dhar's forehead as usual, snapped at Frost in annoyance.

"It's not fair," Denali called from the ground at Dharanidhar's feet. Dharanidhar lifted him up to sit behind Kanvar so the two could talk over the roar of the wind.

"You're not the only one they left behind," Denali said. "I don't know why my father insists I'm too young to fight in this war. He let Raahi go with his father. I *can* fight, and you should see Frost in battle. She's unbeatable. And I don't understand why they had to leave at night, in this storm. It's like they're purposely trying to leave you behind. They can't even claim you're too young."

Kanvar clenched his good hand into a fist. "Kumar Raza, Stonebiter, Bolivar, and Theodoric know you and I can fight. That's not the problem. The problem is, how do you move an army without being seen by Bendyn and Weston? Those Naga guardsmen have gotten too close to discovering us on their own, and now they have reinforcements, ten more Nagas searching every mind of every person in every village and all of Huayna. It's like Khalid knows we're here and is trying to flush us out. The army had to move, and it's a sure bet the Naga guardsmen won't be flying tonight. This storm is the perfect opportunity to get away from Darvat unnoticed, and Bolivar's a good enough seaman he thinks he can ride it out. Dharanidhar and I will fly as soon as the wind dies down."

"You'd better take Frost and me with you."

"And leave Miki here by himself? Who will feed him and brush him and keep him out of mischief?" Kanvar asked.

"Raahi's mother will do it. I've already asked her. You know Tiago adores him."

Kanvar half smiled. Raahi's little brother, Tiago, had spent every moment he could with Kumar Raza's dog. "All right, you can come with us, Denali. But you realize Dhar and I are headed back to Kundiland, not to Varna? We have to harvest more herbs for his medicine before it's time to attack Stonefountain. He only has a few doses left."

"What? No. The jungle's too hot for Frost."

"So is Varna, that's why Kumar Raza arranged for you to stay here with Raahi's mother. You may be grown enough to fight, but Frost is only a wyrmling. Even though she can fight, she's a baby, Denali. She needs to stay here where the climate is good for her."

Denali folded his arms across his chest. "Take us with you. To Kundiland if you must and then to Stonefountain."

Kanvar grimaced. "All right, but we're not going anywhere until the wind dies down."

Early morning gray streaked the sky as Lord Taral and Saanjh landed at the golden palace at Stonefountain. Taral's hands sweated, and if he'd let his fear run unchecked, he and Saanjh would be headed back to Navgarod as fast as Saanjh could fly. They could probably hide for the rest of their lives in the wild mountains of Navgarod and never have to face King Khalid. But Taral had sworn himself into King Amar's service, and though he'd muddled it badly in losing Aadi, he couldn't abandon his other duties to the rightful king.

Striding as quickly as he could through the palace, Taral found Lord Jesson at his desk poring over reports. "My Lord," Taral said. "I hate to bother you so early in the morning. But I have news for the king that is most urgent.

He'll be furious if I don't give it to him immediately. In fact—" Taral gritted his teeth. "He's going to be furious one way or another."

Lord Jesson gave Taral a rueful smile. "You can't begin to know how angry His Majesty is at you. He just told me to hunt you down and bring you to him."

Taral shuddered. "There is no need to hunt. I am loyal to the king and will accept whatever punishment he sees fit for my failures."

"Leave your sword here and come then." Lord Jesson unbuckled his own sword, laid it on the desk and motioned for Taral to do the same. Then he led Taral to the king's wing of the palace and let him into a reception chamber where King Khalid waited for him.

"Your Majesty," Taral dropped to his knees. "Aadi has vanished. Something tore him free of his bonds. I found a trail of water from the river to the room where I held him. It looked as if some serpent came out of the river in the night, clawed him free, and dragged him down into the water. I could find no trace of him, no feel of his mind, nothing. I think he must be dead, drowned. Perhaps his mind was strong enough to summon a lesser serpent to end his life."

Stony-faced, King Khalid lifted his arm to show a gruesome scar where there had not been one the day before. The skin around it was red and swollen. "Aadi is not dead. Not yet. He's working with a Great Black serpent from Kundiland."

Dragonbound IX

Lord Taral's heart twisted with fear. Indumauli had struck the king. Whatever Indumauli and Aadi had been up to, Taral would be blamed and punished for it.

King Khalid's eyes narrowed, and he took a step toward Taral. "The serpent's name is Indumauli. He and that filthy halfblood have freed ten traitorous young gold dragons from my prison. Since the boy was in your care, I hold you responsible. You will make this right, Taral. I raise you to a member of the Elite Guard and task you with hunting them all down. Take whatever men and weapons you need. I want those dragons dead. I want their dragonstones spread before me. And I want the black serpent's hide nailed to my bedroom wall. But I want Aadi alive. Bring him to me so I can prolong his pain and madness forever."

"Yes, Your Majesty," Lord Taral said. "It is an honor to serve. I will bring these traitors to justice."

Lord Taral retrieved his sword from Lord Jesson's office, returned to Saanjh, and urged him into the air.

Saanjh winged above the river that flowed down from King Khalid's palace and out into the rebuilt city of Stonefountain. Lord Taral gazed at the flowing water. *That serpent has to be here somewhere*, Taral said. *He can't hide his mind from me.* And yet, Taral could not sense the creature. Either Indumauli was dead or unconscious. Deep in his heart, Taral feared for both Aadi and Indumauli, but he kept that fear buried and his mind focused on the bloody task Khalid had given him—find and kill Indumauli and the young gold dragons. No doubt, the gold dragons were Aadi's friends from Kundiland. Aadi had found them at last and freed them with Indumauli's help. For that Taral was glad, but he refused to let himself feel that joy. All he felt was anger at losing Aadi to the serpent and an intense vow to bring the traitors to justice.

Saanjh growled. Both he and Taral were certain Khalid was listening in on their conversation. *We're wasting time searching around Stonefountain for the black serpent and Aadi,* Saanjh said. *We can't feel either of them. That means the serpent is probably dead and Aadi drowned. You must leave the search here to someone else and fly after those renegade gold dragons. Every minute we waste searching for Aadi, the traitor dragons get farther away.*

I'm afraid you're right, Saanjh. Set down there, at my brother's house.

Saanjh adjusted his course away from the river toward a mansion tucked up against the mountain. Lord Fistas's home was large, and he'd spared no human labor in rebuilding the elaborate towers and halls.

Brother, Taral called out as Saanjh landed in Fistas's courtyard.

You're up early, Fistas's groggy mind replied. *Go away. Can't you see I'm sleeping here?*

King Khalid has given me an urgent mission, Fistas, with orders to enlist anyone I must to aid me. If I fail, the king will likely execute me, understand? Lord Taral dismounted and headed inside.

Half-dressed, Fistas met him in the hallway. "What have you gotten yourself into?"

"Come on, I'll tell you while you dress." Lord Taral explained to his brother how he'd learned that Aadi was a halfblood and about King Khalid's interest in the boy. How Taral had volunteered to continue Khalid's experiment to see how long Aadi could survive, but a Great Black serpent had freed Aadi from Taral's bonds and the two had stolen into King Khalid's dungeon and freed ten traitorous gold dragons.

"The serpent actually bit the king. Khalid has a terrible scar from it and is furious," Taral said.

"That's what you get for messing around with the king's plaything. Honestly, Brother, that kind of cruelty doesn't seem like you," Fistas said as he dressed.

Sweat slicked Taral's palms. His brother knew him too well and could betray his true nature to King Khalid. Taral clenched his fists and gave his brother a grim smile. "I'll do whatever it takes to get His Majesty's attention. You know I've always aspired to be an Elite Guardsman. I figured using the boy was my best chance. And I was right; King Khalid raised me to the Elite Guard this morning. But I must not fail him. Unfortunately, he has given me two incompatible tasks. I can't chase down the traitor gold dragons and Aadi and the serpent at the same time. Since I have his permission to enlist whatever aid I need, I'm ordering you and the humans you command to take up the search for the serpent while I go after the gold dragons. He wants the serpent dead and skinned, and Aadi brought to him alive. I have my doubts that either still lives, but if you were to catch them, there is a good chance you would join me in the Elite Guard."

Fistas tied his hair back and buckled on his sword. "If that serpent is alive, I'll find him. If he's dead, I'll dredge the entire length of the river for his body and that of the boy. Have no fear." Fistas's pupils constricted like they always did when he set his full focus on a task. His voice was sharp and cold. "Go. Get those gold dragons. I won't fail you."

"I know you won't," Taral said. "Of the two of us, you've always been the better man."

Taral clapped his brother on the arm and returned to Saanjh. "Let's go hunt some dragons," he said as he mounted.

In the dim morning light, Kanvar watched Dharanidhar dive into the heaving water and come back up with a giant dragonfish clenched in his jaws. The wind had died down before sunrise, but clouds still covered the sky and rain drizzled onto the beach. Dharanidhar returned to shore to share his kill with Kivi and Frost.

Denali let out a low whistle of appreciation. "I never could have brought in that big of a fish with my spear and boat back home in the Great North. Blue dragons are amazing hunters."

Kanvar grinned. As long as he stayed warm and dry on the beach, he liked watching Dharanidhar dive into the cold water. Though Kanvar was sometimes jealous that Dharanidhar no longer needed him to see, Kanvar had grown quite fond of the lesser green serpent that had become Dharanidhar's eyes. Kivi didn't like the cold water any more than Kanvar did, and if allowed to get too cold, tended to drift into hibernation.

"Come on," Kanvar told Denali. "If we don't hurry, there won't be any breakfast left for us."

Nonsense, Dharanidhar said, tearing off a chunk of the best meat from the dragonfish and cooking it with his fire for Kanvar. *I would never forget to feed you. It would feel like starving myself.*

The companions ate without talking after that. Kanvar savored the warm, juicy meat while keeping his mind on the lookout for any sense of other Nagas nearby. Trying to feel for the guardsmen while keeping his own mind shielded from them gave him a vague headache. Denali, though he hated it, wore one of the iron helmets. Karishi had fashioned it for him, so it fit well and wasn't too heavy. Like others who wore the helmets, Denali kept his hidden beneath a crocheted woolen hat, so he didn't look as ridiculous as he felt. No one had been able to convince Frost to leave a helmet on, so Kanvar had to keep her mind shielded as well as his own. Not that the Nagas would have any reason to be looking for a baby Great White dragon.

Kanvar. His father's mind, faint and far away, brushed against Kanvar's shields.

Father, Kanvar responded cautiously, fearing the Naga guardsmen might sense his communication with his father.

Amar wrapped shields around their communication and let impressions and images seep into Kanvar's mind. Aadi was within Khalid's grasp at Stonefountain, tormented and dying. The depth of Aadi's pain staggered Kanvar.

I'll go save him, Kanvar whispered.

There may not be anything you can do. Amar spoke quickly. *But I don't want him to die alone. Find him. Bring him to me. Please. I'll meet you on the Varnan coast. I know it will be dangerous for you, but I have no one else I can send.*

I will. The fleet has sailed from here already. Khalid presses us. He hunts us. Somehow he knows we're building an army to destroy him.

He has seen everything in Aadi's mind.

Even the helmets?

Aadi does not know about the helmets. He was never present when we discussed or used them, thank the fountain. But Kanvar, you know too much. You must not be captured.

I will be careful.

With a pained sigh, Amar's mind slipped away from Kanvar's.

Kanvar licked the last of the dragonfish from his fingers and limped over to Dharanidhar. "Did you hear my father?"

Dharanidhar let out a dangerous growl, and fire sparked between his jaws. *We fly to Stonefountain. We must be sure to come upon it at night so I am not seen. Aadi is with this guardsman, Taral, it seems. We'll fly in, snatch Aadi from where he's bound, and get back out before sunrise.*

"Can you fly fast enough?"

I'll fly whether it hurts or not, Dharanidhar snapped. *I won't let Khalid harm Aadi anymore.* Thinking about the oath he'd made to Akshara, the Great Blue Liberator, to defend the world's freedom no matter the cost, Dharanidhar lifted the barrel that held his medicine and gulped it down. Only one barrel remained tied to his neck behind Kanvar's saddle.

"Come on, Denali," Kanvar called. "King Amar has given us a mission, one only you and I can accomplish since everyone else is busy elsewhere."

Denali let out an excited cheer and raced over so Dharanidhar could lift him and Kanvar up to his neck. Kanvar let Denali sit in front of him and buckled the two of them in tightly together. Frost settled onto Dharanidhar's shoulder, and Kivi took his place on Dharanidhar's head.

"Where are we going?" Denali asked as Dharanidhar sprang into the air.

"We're going to Stonefountain," Kanvar said. "To rescue Aadi from Khalid."

Chapter Two

If you were a very frightened young gold dragon, where would you go, Saanjh? Lord Taral asked as Saanjh winged away from Stonefountain.

When threatened, a young gold dragon will always fly toward home, Saanjh answered. *The question is, are they strong enough to make it across the ocean to Kundiland?*

Taral gritted his teeth and urged Saanjh to turn westward, taking the shortest path from Stonefountain to the ocean. Every mile he put between himself and Stonefountain eased the fear that threatened to overwhelm him. Surely King Khalid had better things to do than keep in contact with his mind forever.

As the city fell away behind him, he increased the shields around his thoughts, hoping Khalid would not notice. He craved privacy and solitude. Khalid had not told him what the gold dragons had done to deserve imprisonment or how long he had kept them held captive. If only

Aadi and Indumauli had told Taral what they planned to do, he might have been able to help them.

Or Khalid would have seen the truth in your mind and we'd all be dead, Saanjh pointed out.

Taral shook his head in frustration. *We're in a tight spot here, Saanjh. If Khalid wanted the gold dragons dead, why didn't he send the Naga Guard after them immediately when they escaped? Why wait until morning and send me? Khalid must already suspect I was trying to help Aadi. That's why he gave me this task. If I fail to kill the young golds and the serpent and bring Aadi back to him, he'll know I'm a traitor. But If I do what Khalid orders, I'll betray King Amar.*

I think what is most important is that you do not betray yourself. Some night a hundred years from now, will you regret what you did today?

I'll regret nothing if I'm dead. Taral squinted across the horizon, watching for a strip of blue that would be his first view of the ocean.

Then you should not fear death.

Right. Taral dropped his gaze to the ground, searching for any sign of the young gold dragons. Though storm clouds from the northeast were bearing down on Stone-fountain, the sky above Taral was clear and the sun shone down on the waving grasslands. There was no place here where the young golds could take shelter, but if they were smart enough to land and hold still, they might go un-noticed by anyone searching from the air.

We may not be able to see them, Saanjh said, *but ten unbonded gold dragons could never hide their minds fully from us.*

That was true, but Taral kept his mind safely behind his own shields, unwilling to expose it to Khalid and unsure yet what he would do if he found the young dragons. Herds of trihorns moved across the savannas. The scent of dust and lesser dragonhide lifted on the air. *What are we going to do?* he wondered. *What will we do if we find them? What if we don't?* Saanjh had no answer.

By the time Taral reached the coast, the rain clouds, driven by a stiff wind, had caught up with him. *We should land,* Taral told Saanjh, *rest and think.*

Saanjh spiraled down to the coast where waves crashed against a rocky shore. Just above the tideline, Taral saw a splotch of gold amid the gray stones.

Saanjh?

I see it.

Saanjh dove toward the rocks. As they came down, Taral saw more gold. The young gold dragons had stopped to rest in the sun and fallen asleep, unaware that the coming storm had betrayed their location.

Taral, look at them, they're hardly more than skeletons. They must not have eaten in a long time.

The sight of the stricken children made Taral queasy. Scars from heavy manacles marred their limbs. Their faces were sunken. They looked like fragile seabirds washed ashore. Killing them would be simple. He need only freeze them in place with his mind and strike them down with his sword.

The youngsters startled awake as Saanjh settled to the ground beside them. They squealed in terror and tried to take to the air, but Taral held them in place, reaching out to take a firm grip on them with his mind. He dismounted and strode toward them. *Go back and fetch one of those trihorns*, Taral told Saanjh.

As Saanjh flapped away, Taral wondered what it would take to convince the young ones to eat raw meat. He had no way to cook the trihorn. Already the rain was falling. He'd not be able to light a fire.

Please, the closest dragon whimpered as Taral walked up to him. *Please, let us go.*

Taral run a soothing hand down his shoulder. The dragon shuddered beneath his touch. "It's all right," Taral said in a soft voice. "I'm a friend of Aadi's. I serve King Amar. Let me help you. What is your name?"

The young dragon stared at Taral as if it had not expected to find a friend among the Naga guardsmen. *I'm Jaymon. If you truly serve the king, free our minds. Let us go.*

Taral released Jaymon's mind but not the others. The little ones needed food. He had to keep them here until Saanjh returned with it. "Jaymon, Aadi told me about you. The two of you planned to bond."

We tried. It did not work.

"I'm sorry. Do you know where Aadi is?"

Jaymon shook his head and held out a leather satchel. *He gave me this and told me he and Indumauli would follow us in the water. But the river runs the wrong direction. We had to come this way. There's a kitrat in there. He wanted me to feed it and keep it alive, but I can't even get it to come out for me. It's too frightened.*

Heart dropping, Taral took the satchel he'd given Aadi. If Aadi had given up the kitrat hatchling, then he had nothing left to live for. Taral's fears were true. Aadi was dead.

Will you feed it? Jaymon asked.

Taral swallowed a lump in his throat. "Yes, I'm going to feed all of you and escort you across the ocean to King Amar. Pray he forgives me for doing this instead of the other task he entrusted me with."

Taral knelt and fed the kitrat while he waited for Saanjh to return. The wind increased and rain whipped across the beach. Saanjh landed, carrying a dead trihorn and laid it in front of the young dragons.

Taral tucked the kitrat away and got to his feet. "I know it's not cooked, and it's barbaric to feed off a kill this way," he said to the young dragons. "But if you want the strength to cross the ocean, you must eat." He released the young golds and backed away.

Jaymon pounced with no hesitation. He tore the trihorn into ten parts and handed it out to the others. They ate the meat, bones, skin, and all like savage lesser dragons.

Taral turned away. *This is Khalid's doing,* he said to Saanjh. *He would turn us all into mindless beasts.*

At least you didn't have trouble getting them to eat, Saanjh said. *For my part, I'm hungry, but I think I'll wait until we can have a properly cooked meal.*

Taral agreed. *Besides, a single trihorn isn't that much to be shared among so many.*

I can fetch another one.

No, I think we should fly now while we still can. At least this wind is at our backs. Let's hope it makes the crossing easier for the children instead of harder.

Taral started to mount Saanjh, but a dark spot on the horizon above the water caught his eye. It grew larger as it neared and took on the shape of a majestic dragon. In the haze and rain, Taral could not make out the color until it swept by overhead. It was gold, a young Great Gold dragon, no bigger than the ones that huddled on the beach. The Naga on its back was dressed in gold armor and wore a golden band across his brow.

Your Majesty, Taral called in surprise. What king would risk his own life to fly alone against his enemy?

The young dragon turned back and flapped down to land next to Saanjh. King Amar swept off of his dragon's back and stared in consternation and horror at the dragons on the beach. "Jaymon, Bellori, Fulkshema, Affonaly," he cried out. "What's happened to you?"

King Amar's dragon let out a concerned wail and rushed to his friends.

"Khalid had them imprisoned, but Indumauli took Aadi from me, and they freed the dragons. I——" Taral faltered. "I can't find Aadi now or Indumauli. I think they're both dead. I was just trying to help the young ones get back to you. But . . . Khalid—" Taral broke off and turned away.

King Amar put a hand on Taral's shoulder and led him away from the dragons so they could speak in private. "After I heard from you, I could not rest knowing Aadi was in torment. I came here to get him and take him back with me to Kundiland," Amar said.

"You can't go to Stonefountain; you'll be killed," Taral said in alarm.

"Unfortunately, Rajan agrees with you. He would not let me leave until I swore to wait here on the coast while Kanvar found Aadi and brought him to me. But when I gave Kanvar that task, I thought Aadi was still safely with you." Amar gazed off toward Stonefountain, his heart deeply troubled.

"I'm sorry I failed you, My King. I could not save him, and I cannot return to Stonefountain to try and enlist more guardsmen to your side. Khalid suspects me, I fear, and has set me a terrible task." Taral shuddered and glanced back at the young dragons.

"What would he have you do?" Amar asked. His voice was gentle but thick with grief at the thought of losing Aadi.

Taral licked his lips. "I . . . he's ordered me to kill these young dragons. Every last one of them and bring their dragonstones to him as proof. Also, I must find Indumauli, kill him, and bring Khalid his hide. He wants Aadi returned to him alive, so he can prolong his agony. But I could not search the river for Aadi and Indumauli and come after the young dragons at the same time. Figuring Aadi was already dead, I left my brother to dredge the river while I flew in search of the escaped children. My King, I would not kill them. I could not. You must believe that."

"I believe you, Taral. I've seen into your heart, and I believe you. You'll have to come with me and the young dragons back to Kundiland." King Amar gave Taral's shoulder a squeeze then headed over to his dragon.

We can't leave now, King Amar's dragon said. *You sent Kanvar into Stonefountain to look for Aadi. Kanvar is expecting to meet you here on the coast. He'll come here for you, and you won't be here.*

"Bensharie," King Amar said, pointing to the other young dragons. "Look at them. I can't send them off alone, and I can't let them stay here. If Taral fails to kill them, Khalid will send others to do the job. We must leave now. I'll contact Kanvar and tell him to break off and meet us in Kundiland."

Bensharie ruffled his wings and shook his head. *Just because Lord Taral can't feel Aadi's mind, doesn't mean Aadi is dead. Parmver trained him well. Aadi can shield his mind and possibly Indumauli's as well.*

Taral shook his head. "You don't understand. Aadi was seeking death. He tried to bond with Jaymon and failed. There's no way he could have survived. I know, I—"

Bensharie growled under his breath. *If you won't go back and help Kanvar find him, I'll go to Stonefountain myself, you worthless cowardly Naga. How dare you say Aadi is dead? He's not. He's my friend, and I'll never stop searching for him.*

"Bensharie." Amar put a hand on Bensharie's chest to calm him. "Lord Taral is not afraid to return to Stonefountain, but Khalid is watching him. If Taral finds Aadi, Khalid will know. What's more, Taral can't go back without the dragonstones or Khalid will kill him. Don't you understand? We need to get your friends home to safety. If Aadi and Indumauli risked their lives to free them, we can't leave them here where they could be harmed."

Fine, Bensharie said. *Let's all go back to Kundiland then. I just wish I could think of a safe way for Taral to stay here. His mission is so vital. But don't call Kanvar off. He may yet find Aadi. Just tell him we'll meet him in Kundiland.*

Taral looped the satchel over his head, figuring it would do no good to argue more with the king's dragon or tell him about the abandoned kitrat.

King Amar went to each of the young dragons in turn, murmuring words of encouragement to them and urging them to fly for Kundiland with him. While King Amar talked, Bensharie paced from the tideline to the water and back several times, ruffling his wings in agitation and growling under his breath. Suddenly he lifted his head and let out a bark of laughter.

King Amar spun round to face him. Taral tensed, not finding anything funny about the situation.

"What is it, Bensharie?" King Amar said.

21

Dragonbound IX

Parmver once told me of a ravine on the eastern slope of Stone-fountain. Bensharie fidgeted. *He said the blue dragons carried all the . . . bodies of the dead gold dragons there after the uprising. The Great Blue dragons and the human rebels killed every gold dragon they could find, whether they were bound to a Naga or not. Young and old. He-dragons and she-dragons, all brutally murdered and discarded in the ravine.*

Lord Taral clenched his fists. "Which part of that do you find funny?"

Bensharie cleared his throat. *I don't find any of that funny. What would be amusing would be the look on Khalid's face when you return with ten young dragonstones. If he truly distrusts you, he won't expect you to return with the stones.*

"You want me to desecrate the bodies of the dead?" Revulsion rolled through Taral.

They're dead, have been for a thousand years, Bensharie said. *And I'm sure they would approve of us using their stones to save the young dragons.*

"I don't approve," Taral said. "This is an evil thing. You want me to continue to pretend to embrace Khalid's evil. Do you know what it does to me, to my heart and soul? Khalid probes deep into my mind. I have to lie even to myself to fool him. And if I do get the stones and take them to him, I still have to find Indumauli and Aadi and turn them over to him, dead or alive."

"Lord Taral's right," King Amar said, coming back to Bensharie. "It is too much to ask any man."

It's not too much, Bensharie said. *Not when the need is so great. You have ordered Kanvar to leave the singing stones untouched.*

How then shall we defeat Khalid? You want to win a war, Amar, but you don't want anyone to get hurt. It can't work like that. At least it never has in the stories I've read.

Lord Taral stared hard at Bensharie. "You speak like a grizzled old dragon, not a wyrmling. How do you come by this brutal wisdom?"

Bensharie lifted his head. *I helped Kanvar stop a Great Red volcanic dragon from using Rajan's powers to take control of the human world. Then Kanvar and I flew into the heart of the human armies to save Rajan's life, and together we fought and defeated the Great Red dragon. He and I have flown around the entire world and returned to our home to find Khalid destroying everything we love. I have rescued a village from destruction and defeated Captain Vitra and his dragon in battle. Most gold dragons have spent their lives in blissful comfort at the golden palace. At least they did until Khalid took possession of Devaj. I was never content to just read stories about heroes. I have lived more in my short life than you probably have in your very long one.*

"And most certainly more than I have," King Amar said, putting a hand on Bensharie's shoulder. "I am most honored to have you as my dragon."

You'd be dead twice over if you did not have me as your dragon, Bensharie said. *If Qadim and the dragon hunters hadn't finished you, Captain Vitra surely would have.*

King Amar grimaced.

Lord Taral winced. "Captain Vitra tried to kill His Majesty?"

Bensharie narrowed his eyes. *Vitra tried to strike down King Amar, even knowing he was the rightful king of Stonefountain.*

Lord Taral shook his head in disbelief. "Captain Vitra is stubborn and vain, but I always took him for a good man."

You were wrong, Bensharie said. *Vitra willingly sided with Khalid, and I was forced to kill him to protect Amar's life. Do you see the problem? King Amar, like you, wishes to think all men are good and will, given the choice, embrace peace and freedom. That would be nice, but I don't think that is the case. Some men, it seems, willingly fight to defend evil and tyranny.*

"I do not," Lord Taral said. "But I was fooled by Khalid's lies. Have you seen him? Housed in Devaj's body, he is so fair. He puts on a show of gentleness and goodwill to all but the Elite Guardsmen. Only those that get close to him start to see the evil beneath the smile. But it is those that are close to him that he watches most carefully. He's already beheaded two as traitors, two good men who started to understand the truth and died for it. Most of the Naga Guardsmen see Devaj as the rightful king and follow him, not Khalid. They believe Khalid's lies that Devaj is free and that he willingly seeks Khalid's help to rule Stonefountain. It seems it must be true, because Devaj is so young and inexperienced. How could he rebuild Stonefountain otherwise?"

"Lord Taral," Amar said. "If there are two who saw the truth as well as you, there must be others who will follow me instead of Khalid if they only knew I was still alive. I need you to find them, pull them together, and ready them to answer my call when it comes."

"My King, I will seek the gold dragonstones, return to Stonefountain, and do everything you ask. But you should know Khalid is watching me. If I find those who would follow you, Khalid will find them through me as well. You underestimate his ability to see and control everything in that city." Taral reached for Saanjh's reassuring presence in his mind. They both knew if they returned to Stonefountain they would be going to their deaths.

A dark shadow crossed King Amar's face. "I do not underestimate Khalid. He has reached into my very soul and torn my heart out. I would like nothing better than to melt away into the deepness of the jungle never to face him again. It would be so much easier to run away and leave the world in his hands. In truth, I do not know how we can defeat him without embracing evil as well. But I will not embrace evil, and I will not run. I will stand and face him as I am. I am deeply touched that you are willing to do the same. Do all you can. Find anyone who will side with us and attempt to keep their identity secret from him. It is an onerous task, one I will not force you to do. The choice is yours: come with me now to Kundiland, or go back to Stonefountain."

Shivers prickled Taral's skin. "I will go, My King." Lord Taral bowed, mounted Saanjh, and lifted into the air. Rain stung his face as they strove against the wind to return to Stonefountain.

Chapter Three

Dharanidhar settled onto the eastern coast of Varna as the sun slid down the stormy western sky. His body shook, and he groaned as he sank to his stomach and lowered his head to the ground so Kanvar and Denali could climb from his neck. Kanvar's knees buckled the moment his feet touched the ground. Dharanidhar's attempt to shield the ache in his back legs from Kanvar was failing. Kanvar remained on the ground where he'd fallen. He leaned back against Dharanidhar's neck and shivered. They'd landed on an empty stretch of the coast. A sparse forest of acacia trees provided habitat for an assortment of lesser dragons and a variety of birds, but Dharanidhar made no attempt to hunt.

Kivi let out a petulant hiss. He was hungry and used to being fed.

"Sorry, Kivi." Denali uncoiled the lesser green serpent from Dharanidhar's head and set it in the grass. "If you're hungry, you'll have to hunt your own dinner tonight."

Kivi hesitated for a moment then shot off into the trees after a lizard.

Denali unsheathed his hunting knife. "Guess I'll go see if I can catch something as well. I can't take down anything big enough to feed Dharanidhar, but maybe you and I and Frost will get some food anyway," he told Kanvar.

Frost nuzzled Dharanidhar's chin, burbling in concern.

I'm fine, Dharanidhar grumbled. *I'll hunt my own dinner after I rest a minute.*

Kanvar drew in a breath through teeth gritted against the pain. "Maybe you should take that last dose of medicine now, Dhar."

No. Dharanidhar said. *We'll need it more for the flight into Stonefountain and across to Kundiland. If I were a young dragon, we might try for it tonight. But I'm not. We will sleep here tonight and tomorrow fly as close to Stonefountain as we can get in daylight without being seen. Then tomorrow night I will drink the last dose, and we will go after Aadi.*

"All right. It's the best we can do," Kanvar said. "Let's just hope Aadi survives that long."

Denali's fist tightened on the hilt of his hunting knife. "Aadi is strong. He'll survive."

Dragonbound IX

Flying against the storm, Lord Taral had made little progress toward Stonefountain. As the sun set behind him, he urged Saanjh to the ground. The Savanna grasslands held no shelter from the rain. Taral's vest, silk shirt, and trousers were soaked as if he'd been swimming up a river rather than flying. The bite of the cold rain and the hunger that gnawed at him made him surely, but he politely kept his emotions shielded from Saanjh. Saanjh was hungry too.

Having second thoughts about eating raw trihorn? Saanjh said. *I am.*

Lord Taral shook his head. "Go ahead and hunt if you want Saanjh. Maybe the rain will stop by morning, and we can light a fire to cook it then."

Saanjh lifted Taral from his neck and settled to the ground beside him, using his wing to shelter Taral from the rain instead of going off to hunt.

"Thank you, Saanjh, but I'm pretty well already soaked." Despite that, Taral lay against Saanjh's warm body and tended to the kitrat hatchling.

When he woke in the morning, he was pleased to see the storm had passed.

Taral struggled to light a fire with the damp scrubs and grasses while Saanjh left to hunt. The sun was well up before he coaxed a flame out of the smoldering kindling. Saanjh returned with a dead spine-back raptor and the two puzzled over how to skin and cook it.

"Life was good in Aesir," Taral said as he held a chunk of meat over the fire with his sword and thought of the dozen human cooks that tended to his kitchen back home.

Life was *good*, Saanjh said. *Before the earthquake. Before*—

"Here." Taral gave the cooked meat to Saanjh before thrusting his sword into the ground and stalking off. He could not erase the memory of his wife's lifeless hand sticking out from beneath the white stones of the toppled wall. He was hungry, but there was an emptiness inside him that food would not fill. At least his children still lived. His three daughters and a son were all grown adults and were living at his country estate, safely away from Aesir, when the earthquake hit.

I'm sorry, Saanjh said.

"It's as if the world itself was twisting in agony at the thought of Khalid returning to it, like it knew that everything was about to change for the worse." Taral clenched his fists and stared across the grasslands at the looming mountain that housed Stonefountain. "I wanted to believe that rebuilding Stonefountain was a good and glorious thing. I needed to think that we were doing right by forcing the humans from their homes. Saanjh, what have we been a part of? What evils have we helped perpetrate?"

Saanjh cut a piece of meat for Taral, cooked it on the sword, and brought it over to him. *Eat, the sun is shining. What more can you want from life?*

Taral turned his face toward the warmth of the sun. In the heat of the fire and sunlight, his clothes started to dry. "I want my wife back. I want Kumar Raza and his brother never to have come to Aesir. I want to go home and live in peace."

Well, since you can't have that, you might as well have breakfast and the morning sunlight. Saanjh pressed the hot meat into Taral's hands. The juices trickled between his fingers.

"How about a plate and proper eating utensils," Taral said. "Is that too much to ask for too?"

Saanjh chuckled. *If you want to return to civilization, then stop wasting time and eat. We have work to do.*

"Don't remind me." Taral ate his fill and scrubbed his hands clean in the grass. With breakfast finished, the kitrat fed, and the fire out, Taral climbed onto Saanjh's neck. "Fly around wide, Saanjh, we need to come at the eastern side of the mountain without being seen."

It took until midday for Saanjh and Taral to find the ravine Bensharie had spoken of. It was an eerie place of twisted trees and fallen boulders. The bottom of the narrow ravine was strewn with bones. The bodies of the dragons had long since decayed away, the bones bleached and collapsed. Time had covered them with sand, stone, and grass. But here and there, the bones could be seen sticking up like ghostly memories of the dead, reaching out from their graves in a silent plea not to be forgotten.

Taral shuddered as Saanjh landed and folded his wings.

Finding dragonstones here could take a while, Saanjh said.

"We don't have a while so start digging. Your claws will be a lot more useful than my hands."

Saanjh wrinkled his nose in loathing and began to dig the ground where the closest bone could be seen. Several hours later, Taral tucked the last of the ten small dragon-stones into the satchel with the kitrat.

As disagreeable as disturbing the bodies of the dead to find the stones had been, Taral knew the next part of his job would be worse. Before mounting Saanjh, he knelt on the rocky ground and closed his eyes. Bit-by-bit he recon-structed his own memories—feeling the exhilaration of finding the traitorous gold dragons on the beach, pinning them there, and one-by-one in all the bloody detail, striking them down and prying the stones from their forehead, and enjoying it, reveling in their terror and pain, feeling the hot revenge against those who would rebel against their king, Khalid the Glorious.

Saanjh accepted the bloody images Taral created and made them his own as well. Soaked in the alluring thrall of torture and destruction, Saanjh and Taral winged back to the city.

As they approached, Taral saw Fistas and his men still searching the river. Fistas waved Taral down where a line of boats had cast weighted nets across the river and were dragging the bottom in search of Aadi and Indumauli's bodies.

"Have you found anything yet?" Taral asked as he dismounted.

"Not yet." Fistas looked Taral over and frowned. "You look terrible."

"I was out all night in the storm. How did you think I'd look?"

"Did you have better luck than I have so far?"

Taral clutched the satchel at his side. "I found them."

Fistas scowled. "And?"

"I killed them as Khalid ordered."

Fistas gasped and grabbed his brother's arm. "Taral, they were children."

Taral tore out of his brother's grasp. "They were traitors."

Fistas stared hard into Taral's eyes for a moment before speaking again. When he did, his voice was low and his shields fully up. "I don't like what you're becoming, Taral. I think you should resign from the Elite Guard. Stay as far away from the king as you can. I won't say more. But you need to think about the kind of man you want to be."

Taral sucked in a sharp breath, and his resolve wavered. His brother was the last person he expected to judge him so harshly. "It's not like you've never killed anyone, Fistas. It's not like you have ever been gentle with the humans or withheld your whip from anyone." His words came out hot and angry. "I serve the king. To my dying breath, I do as he commands."

Fistas's face went cold and blank. "Yes, of course. We all do." Fistas drew away and went back to supervising his men.

Taral tasted blood in his mouth and realized he'd bitten his tongue to keep from speaking or even thinking the things he held wrapped so closely to his heart. His hands shook as he climbed back on Saanjh.

"Let's go to the palace and get this over with," Taral said.

Perhaps we should go home so you can clean up and change first, Saanjh said. *Entering the presence of the king in this state would be disrespectful.*

"I don't care." Taral forced himself to breathe evenly and deny the regret he felt about killing the young dragons.

Saanjh's voice rumbled deep in Taral's mind at the center of his shields. *There are no bloodstains on your clothes.*

The rain might have washed them away.

No, Taral. Calm down and do this right. We can deal with your brother later.

I don't want him to think of me this way. Anyone else, I don't care. But not Fistas.

Let it go, Taral. Don't think about it. Focus on the memories you must show Khalid. Saanjh landed in Taral's courtyard and set him on the ground. Saanjh adjusted his speech to a higher level that could more easily be heard by others. *King*

Khalid will be proud of what you've done. Your place in the Elite Guard will be secure.

"Not until we find Aadi and that vile serpent." Taral strode inside to change. Giri, the only human servant he'd kept for himself in this city, met him in his chambers. "I need a hot bath, Giri, and some clean clothes. Quickly."

Giri hesitated, his hands clenched in front of him. "The boy is gone."

"Yes, I know that, Giri," Taral snapped. "Why do you think Fistas and his men have been searching the river?"

Taral set the satchel aside, tore his wrinkled and muddy shirt off, and threw it on the bed.

Giri went into the bathing room to draw his bath. Taral stalked in after him.

"I was hoping you'd be able to heal him," Giri said.

Taral sighed. "So was I, Giri. But he has betrayed the king, and I must find him and bring him to justice. Have you seen him since I've been gone?" Taral combed gently through Giri's memories for any sign of Aadi, but found nothing. Taral broke away from Giri's mind in frustration. For a moment he had hope that Giri knew what had happened to Aadi after the serpent struck Khalid. Perhaps it was best that he didn't. Taral didn't know what he would do if he found Aadi alive. He couldn't possibly give him over to Khalid. But with Khalid watching, Taral would not be able to hide him.

"No, My Lord. I have not seen Aadi."

"If you do, if he comes back here, I must be told immediately, understand?"

"Yes, My Lord."

By the time Taral had bathed, dressed, and eaten a warm meal provided by Giri, he was calmer and more in control. It was time for him to deliver the dragonstones to Khalid and accept the praise he so richly deserved for hunting down the traitor dragons. He left the kitrat hatchling with Giri, took the satchel, and headed for the palace.

He found Khalid holding court, his eyes shining a warm gold to enhance Devaj's good and gentle nature. Wearing glittering gold robes and a golden crown studded with diamonds, Devaj sat on the throne atop a raised dais. Six Elite guardsmen surrounded the foot of the dais, their hands resting surreptitiously close to their sword hilts. Lord Jesson, the captain of the Elite Guard, was not present. The humans and Nagas in the throne room were enraptured by the king and listened approvingly to his commands and judgments.

As Taral waited for his turn to speak, he basked in the king's goodness and glory. He felt blessed beyond measure to witness the return of the rightful king and participate in the rebuilding of Stonefountain. Generations before him and generations to come would all envy his opportunity to serve the shining golden king.

When Devaj's eyes fell upon him, Taral dropped to one knee, lifted the satchel from over his shoulder, and bowed his head.

Devaj rose. "You may all go," he told the on-looking crowd. "We are finished here for the day."

When the crowd had dispersed, Devaj descended the dais with graceful steps. The Elite Guard closed in around him as he reached the base. "Stand back," Khalid snapped. His hand closed around the hilt of his sword. "I'll kill any man who takes a step closer."

The guardsmen moved their hands far from their sword hilts and stepped back.

"Come with me," Khalid ordered Taral and started from the throne room.

Taral rose to his feet to follow.

"Leave your sword," Khalid commanded. His cold voice echoed through the empty room.

Taral unbuckled his sword belt and handed it to the closest guardsman who stood stony faced where Khalid had left him and the others. None made any move to follow their king.

Taral hastened his steps to catch up with Khalid in the hallway headed for his own chambers. "It is the Elite Guard's job to protect you," Taral said. "Surely, none of your own men would lift a weapon against you."

"Fool." Khalid rounded on him and drew his sword. "How do you think I died in the first place?"

"Th-the blue dragons wielding the singing stones?" Sweat broke out on Taral's face and back.

"No," Khalid snarled. "My own guards murdered me in my bed. I woke only long enough to see their faces as they drove a sword through my heart. Do not think for a moment that I will make that same mistake again. I trust no man, Taral. I will never trust again."

Taral licked his lips in fear. Devaj's eyes had gone from glowing faintly gold to burning red with Khalid's rage. "But why?" Taral asked. "Why would anyone do that? You are the king." Taral focused his mind on his own overwhelming adoration of Khalid. In his joy of being accepted into direct service of the king, he could not comprehend how anyone could betray that trust.

Khalid let out a cold laugh and sheathed his sword. "Pretend innocence all you want, Taral. I trust you as well as any other man, which is not at all. But you and I have private business." He motioned Taral into his chambers. "There are some in the Naga Guard who would not understand the necessity of what I asked you to do."

Taral stepped inside and waited for Khalid to come in after him and close the door. "I hope you have not failed me," Khalid said.

"Your Majesty, had I not found the traitor dragons I would still be out looking for them." Taral held the satchel out to the king and opened his mind so Khalid could see Taral's memories of trapping and slaying the young gold dragons.

With Taral's mind open to him, Khalid searched deeper, prying below the memories to see why Taral had been willing to kill the children when other Naga guardsmen might have stayed their hand. He found first Taral's over-whelming fear that he would fail the king and be executed. As loath as Taral might be to kill children, he cared more for his own life than theirs. With a brutal flick of his thoughts, Khalid tore aside Taral's outward fears and stabbed even deeper into his mind. There, Khalid encountered Taral's lifelong desire to qualify for the Elite Guard. The endless extra hours he'd spent training with the sword when most other young men had long since left off. The countless nights he'd stayed up late pouring over his studies, learning anything and everything that might make him stand out from the other young Naga men. He'd applied and been tested for acceptance into the Elite Guard every year for two decades back in Navgarod and always failed by only the slimmest margin. But his long string of failures had only hardened his resolve to someday succeed and join the Elite Guardsmen he so admired.

Khalid chuckled and withdrew, leaving Taral gasping. "I suppose you've finally got what you wanted," Khalid said in a mocking voice.

Taral squeezed his eyes closed and tried to fight back the dizziness and nausea from Khalid's brutal invasion of his mind. He heard the dragonstones tumble out of the satchel onto a table and opened his eyes to watch Khalid fondle them.

"Your work is not done, you realize," Khalid said, lifting each of the stones to examine them.

"Yes, Your Majesty. I have yet to find Aadi and the serpent. But I will never stop looking for them, however long it takes," Taral said. "You gave Aadi into my care, and I want to finish what I started with him."

"Aadi is mine, not yours," Khalid said.

Taral bowed. "As you command."

Khalid laughed. "I have much more important work for you than such amusements. You do not think that my own men would betray me, but you are wrong. I can sense their minds lurking in shadows, flitting away from my own when I search for them. There are Naga Guardsmen here in the city planning a rebellion against me. You will find them, Taral, and hand them over to me. Do you understand?"

"Yes, My King, I understand clearly. I will not fail you. Thank you for letting me join the Elite Guard at long last. I am grateful beyond words." Taral bowed again, and at Khalid's command retreated from the chamber.

He said nothing to the other Elite Guardsmen as he retrieved his sword and nothing to Saanjh as they flew home through the gathering darkness of night. He left Saanjh in the courtyard, locked himself in his room, and paced. He'd killed the young dragons. Murdered them in cold blood and taken their dragonstones. Shaking hard and blinded by his own disgust at what he'd been forced to become to hide his allegiance to King Amar, he retrieved the halfblood dagger from the place he had hidden it after freeing the spirits of the halfbloods who had been trapped within. Bensharie and King Amar asked too much of him. He couldn't do this, couldn't live while playing such an evil part.

He opened the silver box and lifted the dagger. The dark magic wrapped around his hand and shivered up his arm, calling him to a peaceful repose.

Don't do it, Saanjh said.

You can't stop me.

I can try. Saanjh grappled with Taral's mind until he gained enough control to stop Taral's hand from lifting the dagger to his heart.

Release me, Taral said. *I can't do what King Amar wants now, not when Khalid has given me the very same task. If I find the rebel guardsmen, Khalid will kill them, and they will be no use to King Amar when he needs them.*

You don't know that. You have tricked Khalid so far. You can continue to do so.

Taral shuddered and gagged. Sure he would never be free now of the lies he'd planted in his own mind. He lived a double life now, and the evil threatened to overwhelm whatever good he may once have had.

"Let me go," Taral cried aloud, struggling to regain control of the hand that wielded the dagger.

Saanjh's control started to slip. *Fistas*, Saanjh called low and shielded into Fistas's mind. *Your brother's life is in peril, come quickly. I do not think I can save him alone.*

Chapter Four

Khalid chuckled as the door closed behind Taral. "What are you up to, Amar?" he said, fingering the gold dragon-stones. "I sense your presence in Taral but buried so deep I might have to destroy his mind to get to it. And what use would he be to me then?" Khalid moved to the open window and stared out across the darkened sky toward Kundiland. Curled up near the far wall, Elkatran watched him with vacant eyes, a testament to Khalid's ability to obliterate the mind of any man or dragon.

"I know you're planning to overthrow me, Amar." Khalid continued talking out loud as if his enemy were present in the room. "I know you're building an army with General Chandran in Maran and the dragon hunters of Daro. Kumar Raza is out there somewhere and Kanvar as well. In Darvat, no doubt, still seeking the singing stones from the Hall of Raahi's Ancestors. But you won't get them. . . . Theodoric, now there's a piece I don't know how you will bring into play. And Rajan." Khalid's skin prickled. He'd aspired to gain much power in his life, any and all he could take hold of and use, but bonding one of his children with a Great Red volcanic dragon had never once entered his mind. Of course not, he'd been a purist back then. Only Nagas and gold dragons were compatible, or so he'd thought. No longer. Perhaps he would arrange for Devaj's first born son to bond with a red dragon. So much fire, so much power. That was something he could control and use, something better than Devaj's weak goodness.

A knock sounded at the door.

Khalid drew his sword. "Enter."

Hands up where Khalid could see them and know he carried no weapon, Lord Jesson slid into the room. His face was pale, and fear curled through his mind.

"From the look in your eyes, I see you've failed me," Khalid said.

"Your Majesty, I personally searched every mind in Daro and found not even the first trace of a rebellion. No one knows anything about an army. How could humans possibly hide an entire army from us? I've met with my men from Darvat and Maran as well. It is the same everywhere. No whisper. No thoughts. Nothing like what you say has to be there. I-I'm not saying you're wrong. You must be right. And there are all the disappearances yet to account for. People vanishing, body and soul. Your Majesty, it's as if they are dead. But what could Amar possibly gain from killing off the humans?"

Khalid swung his sword in an arc and watched how the lamplight glinted off the blade. "Every human dead is one less we can use against him. But it is not like Amar to think of such a thing. Or Theodoric."

"Kumar Raza and Rajan?"

"No. There is something deeper going on here, Jesson." Khalid sheathed the sword and strode over within arms-length of Jesson. "And since you and your men can't seem to discover what it is, I'll have to look into it myself. Unfortunately, Devaj needs to stay here. The king of Stonefountain can't go missing." Khalid reached out and pressed a hand against Jesson's chest.

"Wh-what are you doing?" Jesson backed away, but Khalid followed him, pressing him up against the wall.

"Don't fight me, Jesson. It will hurt a lot less that way."

Despite Khalid's warning, Jesson struggled beneath his hand. Khalid grabbed hold of Jesson's mind and crushed it so there would be no resistance as he slid from Devaj's body into Jesson's.

Jesson let out a single agonizing scream as Khalid took him. Then Jesson's body was fully under his control. Khalid took a deep breath, savoring Jesson's vitality and strength. Devaj had grown weak, and Elkatran useless.

In Jesson's chamber, Jesson's dragon trumpeted in fear.

Silence, Khalid told it, *unless you want to end up like Elkatran.*

The dragon fell silent and made no attempt to fight Khalid as Khalid took control of his mind as well.

"Khalid." Devaj spoke from the floor where he'd crumpled when Khalid left his body. "Leave Jesson and his dragon alone. Am I not enough for you?"

"You are a useless weakling." Khalid kicked him in the stomach and watched him curl up in pain. "But I still need you. Stay in this chamber until I return. Speak to no Naga. Tell the servants you are sick and not to be disturbed. I'll be watching you, Devaj. You know distance cannot separate our minds. Do not try to double-cross me, or I'll punish you like you cannot imagine."

Devaj moaned and remained curled in his place on the floor as Khalid left the room, summoning Jesson's sword, and calling mentally for Jesson's dragon. Khalid had work to do. He would not sit passively while Amar plotted his overthrow. Within minutes, Khalid had left the palace and was flying full speed toward Kundiland.

Taral fought his way free of Saanjh's control only to be pinned by a new force, dark and faceless and more powerful than any single Naga. The combined power of an unknown number of shielded Nagas locked Taral in place. He waited, panting in his darkened chamber, straining to make out who held him captive but unable to do so. He did not fear, for he'd already decided that death was his only escape. Nothing his unknown captors could do to him would be worse than what he'd already done to himself.

The handle of his chamber door jiggled, but whoever was trying to enter found it locked. Was it Giri? Taral wondered what Giri would do when his master was gone. The lock snapped open, manipulated by Naga power, and Fistas slid into the room, closing and locking the door behind him.

"Fistas." Taral's voice came out in a strained whisper as he tried to warn his brother to flee before whatever force that held Taral bound captured Fistas as well.

"It's all right, Taral." Fistas crossed the room and pried the dagger from Taral's hand. As the caress of dark magic spun up Fistas's arm, he dropped the dagger, cursing. "What is that? Where did you get it?"

"Khalid." Taral remained frozen in place. Only his voice worked.

"I told you to stay away from him." Fistas's voice was filled with cold hatred. "But don't worry. We are going to free your mind from his control. I don't like the things he's making you do."

"We?" Taral was sure it was a unified group of powerful Nagas that held him bound. "Who is holding me? What do you have to do with them?" Taral asked.

"You will never know who any of them are," Fistas said, forcing Taral to the bed and making him lie down. "We keep our identities shielded even from each other. Now be still and let me help you." Fistas pressed his hand against Taral's forehead and tried to enter his mind.

"No, don't!" Taral cried out. He did not want his brother to see the lies he'd invented for Khalid. "Leave me alone, Fistas, please. Just leave me alone."

"I'm your brother," Fistas said. "I'm not going to let that demon destroy you."

Taral shuddered. Alone, his brother would never have the power to enter Taral's mind against his will. But Fistas was not alone, and the other men who held him blasted his shields away, leaving his mind open for his brother to see the horrors that Taral had planted there.

Fistas pushed aside Taral's memory of murdering the young gold dragons and pressed deeper, trying to find the compulsion Khalid must have planted in Taral's mind to make him behave so cruelly. He found only Taral's irredeemable ambition. Taral would do anything, even brutally kill the children, to secure his place in the Elite Guard.

"Brother, what kind of monster are you? All my life I looked up to you, never thinking I could be as good a man as you were, but it was all a lie," Fistas said.

His hurt accusation was more than Taral could bear. "Kill me, Fistas. Let me die."

No, Saanjh said. He tore aside all of the careful lies Taral had constructed and bared the center of Taral's soul to his brother and the other nameless Nagas whose minds held him. Fistas gasped as everything Taral had seen in Aadi's mind spread out before him, followed by Taral's memory of meeting King Amar on the coast.

You say you wish to kill Khalid, Saanjh said. *Then you are the men His Majesty Amar has sent us to find. Alas, Khalid has also sent us to find you and turn you over to him.*

"King Amar is alive," Fistas said in lost astonishment. "We never dreamed. We planned only to kill Khalid so we could return to Navgarod as free men."

Taral groaned as his memories of the brutal slaughter of the young gold dragons faded into the truth of their rescue. "Brother, you know I would never kill any child. Please, believe me. I am working for King Amar." He could only hope the combined power of the minds of Fistas's allies would shield the truth from Khalid.

Fistas gave his brother a rueful smile. "Of course you wouldn't kill anyone. I'm sorry I doubted you, but you have to admit your lies are very convincing. It seems you had even convinced yourself. But we have a problem now." He patted Taral's shoulder and paced across the darkened room. "Whatever King Amar plans to order us to do, those orders will come through you, but we can't let you remember anything about us or your meeting with King Amar. You are too close to Khalid, and he already hunts us. And why you thought killing yourself would solve the problem, I don't know. You *must* remain alive. It appears King Amar is relying a great deal on whatever aid we can give him."

Taral struggled to free himself from the minds that held him. "I was overcome with the lies I had told myself. I had to believe them for Khalid to believe as well."

"It's a good thing Saanjh called me to come stop you. Your ability to weave the most detailed false memories is amazing."

Taral moaned. "What choice did I have?"

"None." Fistas strode back over to the bed and pressed his hand against Taral's forehead once more. "And I have no choice but to reconstruct your lies and erase this encounter from your mind and Saanjh's, as well as Aadi's memories and the truth that you serve King Amar. But don't despair, I'll leave a trigger. When King Amar contacts you with his commands, then and only then, will you remember that you work for him and must pass his commands on to me. And, dear brother, I think we must also erase your desire to kill yourself. You must believe you enjoy the imaginary life you've created for yourself. You must remain pleased to be doing Khalid's dirty work until the time is right for us all to turn against him. I only hope it will come soon."

"Fistas." Taral grabbed Fistas's wrist. "If you do this, I might actually . . . hurt someone. I could never live with myself if I did. Promise me you won't let me hurt any innocent human or dragon."

Fistas sucked in a pained breath. "I promise. I may care nothing for the pathetic humans, but I know you do. I won't let you hurt them."

Taral swallowed the lump in his throat and let his mind and body relax. The combined power of the shielded Naga minds swept over him along with his brother's.

He woke later, alone in his chamber, with the strange feeling that he'd meant to do something, but couldn't remember what it was. When he rose from the bed, his foot brushed against the halfblood dagger where it lay on the floor. Strange, how had it gotten there? He picked it up and tucked it into a loop on his belt.

Saanjh, he said to his dragon who had curled up in the courtyard. *What's going on? I fell asleep. Weren't we supposed to be doing something?*

Saanjh's mind came back in a groggy rumble. *Mmmm. It's the middle of the night. I don't think there's much we can do at the moment. In the morning we need to resume the search for Aadi and Indumauli. And, of course, we must begin to uncover the traitors among the Nagas before they move against His Majesty.*

Taral rubbed his head. It hurt for some reason. He wandered out to the courtyard to stare into the river water that rippled past. "We're going to find that mewling half-blood and make him pay for betraying the king."

Yes, Saanjh agreed. *I have no doubt we'll find both him and the serpent. If Fistas and his men are too incompetent to catch them, you can be sure we will.*

Kanvar breathed a sigh of relief as the medicine spread through Dharanidhar's aching bones. Earlier in the day they'd landed on the northern slope of Mt. Stonefountain and taken shelter beneath a rocky overhang that hid their presence from any Nagas and dragons in the air. Night's darkness had come at last. Dharanidhar stretched and sharpened his claws on the rocks. Denali was buckled on Dhar's back with Kanvar.

Kanvar shifted uncomfortably. "I don't think this is going to work, Dhar. I can't reach my crossbow tucked in this tight with Denali. Can you carry him in one of your foreclaws?"

I might need my claws to fight. We are flying into the center of our enemy's stronghold, Dharanidhar said.

"That's what I'm saying, Dhar. I need to be able to use my weapons."

"Me too," Denali said, trying to reach for a pair of iron spears strapped one on either side of Dharanidhar's neck. If he weren't buckled in with Kanvar, he would have easily been able to draw the weapons.

Fine. Dharanidhar waited for Denali to unbuckle and grab the spears then took him in his foreclaw. *But I think my claws would be better used for fighting than carrying a scrawny boy with a couple of sticks. This is suicide, you realize. If anyone notices us, we have little chance of escape. We'll have to make sure we die fighting before Khalid can pry what we know from our minds.*

Kanvar rebuckled himself, pulled out his crossbow and loaded it. "You're right on that account, Dhar, but I don't think it will come to that. No one knows we're coming. We're flying in under cover of darkness. It's far less crazy than what Bensharie and I did to rescue Rajan from the Maranies."

And how do you propose we find Aadi? Dharanidhar asked.

Kanvar grimaced. His father had contacted him earlier in the day with the fell news that Aadi was no longer with Taral and had last been seen with Indumauli. Both Amar and Taral strongly feared Aadi was dead, probably Indumauli as well. Only Bensharie insisted otherwise.

"I'm with Bensharie on this one," Kanvar said. "Aadi is too stubborn to die, and Indumauli would never fail Amar by letting him. Taral said he couldn't feel Aadi and Indumauli, but Taral only looked close to the city. Indumauli is a fast swimmer. He may have reached the southern coast of Varna before Taral even started looking for him, which means they could be halfway across the ocean to Kundiland by now."

"Then why have we come to Stonefountain?" Denali called up to him from Dharanidhar's claw. Frost chirped in agreement.

Kanvar winced at how loud Denali had to talk to be heard from Dharanidhar's claw. They needed silence, but Kanvar couldn't hear Denali's thoughts while he wore the iron helmet. If they had to talk now, out loud was the only option. Kanvar rested his crossbow across his lap and asked Dharanidhar to lift Denali up closer to his head so they could speak quieter. "Because Amar can't feel Aadi and Indumauli either, and he knows them better than anyone. If they were indeed out of range of the minds of the Nagas at Stonefountain, Amar would most likely have found them. But he can't search minds here very well without someone noticing. The truth is, we don't know where Aadi and Indumauli are. Assuming they're alive—which I'm counting on—they're either safely on their way home and don't need our help, or they've gone to ground somewhere along the river, and the Naga Guardsmen have them pinned so they can't escape. If they're pinned, we need to find them and get them out. The only thing to do is go over the mountain and have a look."

Dharanidhar pushed off into the air with Kanvar riding on his neck, Frost clinging to his shoulder, and Denali in his foreclaw. Kivi hissed from his usual place curled up on Dharanidhar's forehead.

Good thing Kivi sees better in the dark than you do, Kanvar, Dharanidhar said as he tilted away from a looming precipice and came around the shoulder of the mountain. Kanvar shuddered. His night vision had always been horrible.

Dharanidhar winged over the crest of the mountain and Stonefountain came into view below them. Kanvar sucked in a surprised breath. The city was no longer an empty ruin. Lamps lit broad streets and spacious mansions.

Even in the night, the city was stunningly clean and beautiful, like nothing Kanvar had ever seen before. His heart swelled and a lump formed in the back of his throat. The same feeling of wonder and joy he'd experienced when Khalid had returned the singing stones to Stonefountain washed over Kanvar now.

Dharanidhar, look at it, Kanvar said, hardly able to speak. *Look what Khalid has done, what he's built.*

Dharanidhar clenched his jaws to keep from letting out a furious roar and filling the sky with blue fire. *Khalid didn't build this; human and dragon slaves did, some from our own pride, Anilon among them.* His anger tore through Kanvar, shattering his initial awe.

Sorry, Dhar, he murmured. *I just didn't expect it to look so beautiful.*

Look to the river, Dharanidhar said. *There are boats all over it and soldiers with lanterns lining the banks from the base of the waterfall as far as I can see.*

Kanvar tore his eyes away from the beautiful streets and buildings and glanced down at the dark water. Dharanidhar was right.

They're looking for them, Dhar said. *A thousand soldiers searching for Aadi and Indumauli, how could they possibly have not found them?*

Kanvar stared at the flurry of lights across the water and along the riverbank and chuckled. *Yes, they're looking, but not a one of them has any sense. They'd have been better off sending out a single dragon hunter than the Naga Guardsmen and human soldiers.*

Dragonbound IX

Kanvar shared his memory with Frost and Dharan-idhar of a simple hunt he'd gone on with Kumar Raza and Raahi. Kumar Raza had led the hunt for a lesser black serpent, but he'd not taken the two boys to the river bank to stare into the water, hoping to catch sight of the serpent. Instead he'd walked them a ways away from the water, paralleling the river until he'd found a mound of springy ground. Then he'd sent Kanvar to the water's edge and had Raahi drive a spear into the ground where they stood. The serpent had been holed up in its lair where Raahi thrust his spear. The attack on the lair had sent the serpent zipping out into the water where Kanvar's crossbow bolt had finished it off.

Those soldiers and Nagas know nothing about black serpents, Kanvar said. *Fortunately we do. I'm going to need your help though, Frost. Indumauli's lair could be anywhere on either side of the river from the waterfall, clear out to the ocean. There are a lot of mansions along the water front near the falls. I could be wrong, but I don't think he'd be able to dig a lair beneath them without being discovered. So, it's likely to be a little bit farther downriver. Dhar-anidhar and I will fly low along the east side of the river. Frost, you fly along the west. Indumauli is a lot bigger than that lesser black serpent I hunted. Look for a mound or some other formation that might indicate a lair beneath it. Stay away from the soldiers and the lights. We don't want to be seen. Wait, Frost, let Denali put his knit cap over your head before you go down there. We can't have anyone seeing the glow of your dragonstone.*

Frost grumbled in annoyance, but flapped down to Denali, snatched his hat, and shoved it down over her dragonstone. By the time she'd finished, Dharanidhar had moved out from the center of the city and reached the point where the buildings gave way to farm fields.

Frost flew to the right of the river, and Dharanidhar dropped down on the left. There was noise, light, and commotion along the banks and on the water as the boats dragged the river bottom and the soldiers stood ready to attack the Great Black serpent if it should be scared up from the water. But everyone's attention was on the water and not the land behind them.

Kanvar couldn't see well in the dark, and Dharanidhar couldn't see at all. They both relied on Kivi's sight. With a smug hiss, the lesser green serpent scanned the ground. Scattered trees grew along the riverbank, but the ground beyond them was flat and tilled. Wheat stalks bent in the wind of Dharanidhar's passing. Kanvar's heart began to knot up. All the ground was tilled and planted, leaving no-where Indumauli could have made a lair undisturbed. The farther they got from the city, the more Kanvar's hopes began to sink. He sent his mind out searching for Aadi and Indumauli but felt nothing.

Turn back, he told Dhar as they flew past where the last brigade of soldiers was searching. *If they've made it this far, they'll be out to the ocean already. If they're pinned, it will be back where the soldiers are looking.*

Dharanidhar swung around and started flying back the way they'd come. *Have you seen anything, Frost?* Kanvar asked the baby white dragon. Frost was so much smaller than Dharanidhar, she had not covered as much ground as he had and was still far back along the shore.

I hate this hat, Frost said. *It itches.*

Leave it on, Kanvar ordered. *Are you looking? Do you understand what we're searching for?*

There are lights on the water.

Frost, Kanvar said. Dharanidhar rumbled in annoyance and flew across the river, making his way back up the opposite side.

Frost settled to the ground on top of the rubble of an ancient fallen mansion and stared at the glimmering lanterns on the boats.

Kanvar sucked in an excited breath. *That's it, has to be. She's found it. That mansion is just the right distance from the water. There's nothing left above ground but a pile of boulders and dirt, but if it had storerooms below it, they might still be intact, or a portion of them at least.*

Dharanidhar rumbled in agreement and sped upriver to where Frost had landed. Flapping gently, Dharanidhar settled to the ground on the opposite side of the ruin from the river.

Come down off the top of the rubble, Frost, Kanvar called to the white dragon. *You could be seen up there.*

Frost let out a low whine as a bright white lantern lifted into the air in the hands of a Naga guardsman atop his dragon. *Mama*, she cried and sprang into the air after it. If Kanvar hadn't been shielding her mind, the guardsmen would certainly have heard her.

Dharanidhar dumped Denali on the ground, sprang into the air, and caught Frost in his cupped foreclaws.

Mama, Mama, Mama, Frost cried.

Dharanidhar settled to the ground again and hunched down behind the fallen mansion. Kanvar kept Frost's mind as well as his own and Dharanidhar's locked behind a tight shield as the Naga and his dragon flew along the river toward the palace.

Dharanidhar set Frost on the ground next to Denali who dropped his spears and grabbed her.

That was too close, Kanvar said to Dharanidhar as he freed himself from his saddle and let Dharanidhar set him on the ground.

Frost let out an unhappy moan.

"What's wrong with her?" Denali asked. "I can't feel her thoughts with this stupid helmet on."

"She was calling for her mother," Kanvar said.

Denali hugged Frost and stroked her wings, whispering, "That wasn't your mother, Frost. It was just a lantern. It's all right. I'm here with you, and so is Dharanidhar. He's your father now, remember, I told you he is. We're your family, Frost. You're not alone."

Chapter Five

Denali kept his arms around Frost, trying to sooth her. She'd never acted this way before, never called out for her mother. Her scales were smooth and chilly beneath his fingers. After her time with Vasanti, Frost must have started to realize there was a female presence missing from her life, and the cold white light of the lanterns had stirred something in her.

"It's the lantern that Naga had," Denali whispered to Kanvar who was limping along the edge of the rubble, looking for an opening down into Indumauli's lair. "It didn't flicker. There was no flame in it, just like a white dragonstone."

Kanvar came back over to Denali. "There's a light like that in Parmver's lab, remember?"

Denali nodded. "I think she has a natural instinct to fly toward her mother's light."

"I'm sorry, Frost. Your mother isn't here." Kanvar rubbed Frost's neck. Frost's parents had died of starvation before she'd hatched. Denali had meant to explain it to Frost, but Frost had not seemed old enough yet to understand. "Why don't you and Frost help me look for a way underneath this mound?" Kanvar said. "We're dangerously exposed here and need to move quickly."

"Come on, Frost," Denali said, taking her foreclaw and leading her over to the rubble. "We need to find our friend, Aadi. Can you smell him? Can you feel him?"

Dharanidhar shifted uncomfortably, and Denali figured his back legs must be hurting him, hunched down as he was. But if he straightened, his head and shoulders would stick up over the mound where people on the river could see it if they gazed off into the dark landscape.

There was a faint throb of light beneath the knit cap on Frost's head. Denali bit his lip and tried not to be too annoyed. Losing his fuzzy connection with Frost's mind was the worst thing about wearing the iron helmet. He couldn't tell what she was saying to him. She pulled away and began sniffing and scrabbling around the base of the mound.

"It has to be around here somewhere," Kanvar whispered. "I doubt any black serpent would have a lair with only one way in and out."

"Both openings might be under water though," Denali said, keeping his voice low. "Too bad we can't ask Aadi. He's the one that was always hanging out by the underground lake with Indumauli."

Frost let out a chirp, clawed at the ground, and vanished. Denali rushed over to where she'd been and found a small opening, barely big enough for the little dragon to slip into, and maybe Denali.

Denali stuck his head in and with a good deal of wriggling managed to get his shoulders through. Up ahead he could see the faint glow of Frost's dragonstone beneath the knit cap. Everything else was black earth.

"Take the hat off, Frost," he called softly. The light got brighter but didn't help much. Above, below, and close on both sides was dirt and rocks. To move forward at all, Denali had to drag himself on his stomach. I'm going to suffocate and die, Denali thought to himself. When Frost's light disappeared suddenly, he wanted to yell for Kanvar to grab his legs and pull him back out, but when he kicked his feet, he realized there was no longer open air around him. He'd gone too far to get any help back out.

Gritting his teeth, he dragged himself forward in the dark. The rough dirt tore at his clothes and rubbed his hands, elbows, and knees raw. Just when he thought he would be buried alive in the narrow space, the ground gave out in front of him, and he slid forward into a low cellar. Water covered three-quarters of the floor. Frost sat in the mud at the edge of the water, clutching the knit cap in her foreclaws. Her stone glowed a pale white, and she licked the face and neck of a bedraggled form lying limp in the mud.

"Aadi." Denali bolted forward and dropped to his knees beside his friend to get a better look. Aadi's eyes were closed, his gray skin sunken. His chest rose and fell in shallow breaths. "Aadi, wake up." Denali shook him gently.

"I'm awake," Aadi murmured. "Put out the light. It hurts my eyes. What kind of spirit are you, trying to disturb my focus? Can't you see I'm trying to shield myself and Indumauli?"

"I'm not a spirit," Denali said, shaking Aadi again. "Aadi, come on, open your eyes. I'm Denali. Kanvar's here too. We've come to take you to Kundiland."

"You must be a ghost. I can't feel your presence." Aadi rolled on his side and pressed his hands over his eyes.

"I'm not a ghost, Aadi. Here, you can feel me." Denali grabbed Aadi's hand and rubbed it against his own face

Aadi pulled away and curled into a ball. "Don't distract me. I'm too weak to keep fighting this. There are so many soldiers, so many Nagas looking for us."

Frost let out a burble of concern.

"No, Aadi. Look at me," Denali said.

Aadi refused to move or open his eyes.

Denali stood up and glanced around the chamber for Indumauli. He saw no sign of the serpent. "Indumauli," he called softly. "Kanvar's here. We have to go."

A faint ripple moved across the water, but Indumauli remained out of sight. Frost flapped over to Denali and rubbed her foreclaw against the iron helmet.

"I can't take it off, Frost. Kanvar would kill me. Every Naga in Stonefountain might feel my presence. I'm not that good at shielding my mind."

Frost bared her icicle teeth, grabbed the base of the helmet, and tore it off Denali's head.

Aadi gasped and jerked upright, glancing around him.

Denali snatched the helmet from Frost and shoved it back on his head just as Aadi caught sight of him in the light of Frost's dragonstone.

"Denali," Aadi said, shocked. "I thought you were a dream. You have to be. There's no way you could be here in Stonefountain, no way you could have found me."

"You're right," Denali said. "There's no way *I* could have found you, but Kanvar's a pretty good dragon hunter, and Frost is good at burrowing, though I'm betting she'd prefer to do it in snow rather than dirt."

Waves lapped the edge of the pool, and Indumauli slithered out of the water. Indumauli's stone flashed as he said something.

"I'm sorry. I can't hear you," Denali said.

"Why?" Aadi asked. "Why can't we feel you? I sensed your presence for a moment, and then it was gone."

"No time to explain right now. Kanvar and Dharanidhar are waiting up there. They'll be noticed if we don't hurry." Denali went back to the edge of the chamber and peered up at the hole in the wall where he'd come through. He glanced back at Indumauli. "You're not going to fit through that, are you?"

Indumauli hissed and coiled up to the spot. He stuck his head in and a moment later had it wide enough his whole body slid into the opening and vanished.

"Thank goodness he's making it bigger," Denali said. "I really didn't want to try to crawl back through that." He motioned for Aadi to go next.

Aadi glanced around the lair, shuddered once, then followed Indumauli out.

"You go next, Frost," Denali said. "That way I can follow your light."

Frost licked Denali's face and went into the hole.

A few minutes later, Denali came out into the open night air. He heaved a sigh of relief and brushed the dirt out of his hair and face. As soon as he had retrieved his spears from the ground where he'd left them, Dharanidhar snatched him up in his foreclaw. Then Dharanidhar lifted Aadi in his other claw. Indumauli climbed onto Dharanidhar's back and held on like a wyrmling clinging to his mother. Kanvar was already in the saddle once again holding his loaded crossbow. Frost stuffed the knit hat back down over her dragonstone and flapped to Dharanidhar's shoulder. With a soft grunt, Dharanidhar pushed himself off from the ground and took flight.

The moment Dharanidhar lifted off from the ground, Kanvar realized they'd made a mistake. Kanvar had been so focused on getting Aadi, he'd forgotten to keep his mind aware of the Nagas and soldiers. Dharanidhar rose into the air right in front of the Naga guardsman with the lantern whom they'd seen earlier. The Naga's dragon hovered just above the fallen mansion on the river side and had his attention focused in the spot where Dharanidhar came up as if the guardsmen had heard something and come to investigate.

The lantern flashed across Kanvar's face and Dharanidhar's head and chest. Kanvar leveled the crossbow at the Naga, ready to shoot if the Naga tried to reveal their presence to his friends.

The light snapped out.

What is it, Fistas? some other Naga called out to the one Kanvar faced.

Fistas chuckled. *Nothing more than a winged raptor, probably lured off the savanna by our lights. I'll take care of it. Keep searching.*

Yes, sir.

The conversation with the other Naga broke off, and Fistas made contact with Kanvar's mind. *Get out of here, Your Highness. Taral said you'd be coming, but I didn't want to believe him. You must be ten times insane to fly this close to Stonefountain. Go now, quickly. Tell His Majesty Amar that Taral has accomplished the task he set for him. We wait here for the king's command.*

Dharanidhar spun away and winged for the coast, pushing himself hard, knowing he and Kanvar would regret it later, but that made little difference now. They'd been lucky, but that luck wouldn't hold if they were spotted again. And they had to get to the ocean before sunrise, or Indumauli would fry on Dharanidhar's back.

Despite Dharanidhar's efforts, the sun was already pushing into the sky by the time they reached the coast. Indumauli's claws had dug deeper into Dharanidhar's scales as the sky grew lighter, but the serpent made no sound or complaint. In fact, Kanvar found Indumauli's mind as tightly shielded as Aadi's. Both were totally closed to him. He had been unable to sense either mind back at the lair, even knowing they had to be there after Frost and Aadi went down in, and Kanvar could see Aadi in Frost's mind.

Kanvar rubbed his head. Either he was too tired and distracted by Dharanidhar's pain, or Aadi was somehow shielding Indumauli as well as himself.

With a groan, Dharanidhar settled into the ocean out past the break line.

"Sorry it's salt water," Kanvar told Indumauli, "but it's better than nothing."

Indumauli slid off Dharanidhar's back and plunged into the water, diving deep where the sun couldn't touch him.

Lift Aadi up here with me, Kanvar told Dharanidhar. *I need to make sure he's all right while you rest.* Kanvar had been deeply disturbed by the sense of Aadi's suffering he'd gotten from Amar's mind. It wasn't fair. If anyone deserved to be a Naga, it was Aadi. Aadi had spent his whole life studying with Parmver, learning everything about Naga history and power. No one wanted it more and knew better what to do with it than Aadi. And yet some cruel twist of fate had made him a halfblood like Kumar Raza: able to sense the dragons, but unable to bond.

We can't rest for long, Dharanidhar said, lifting Aadi up to his neck. *If I don't fly again soon, I won't fly at all. I've got to make it to Kundiland before the medicine wears off completely.*

Kanvar unbuckled, pulled Aadi tight against his chest, and secured both of them down together. Aadi's skin was cool and clammy, his breathing shallow. His eyes were closed tight against the brightening sunlight. He made no move to resist Kanvar's hold on him and little effort to sit upright on his own.

"Aadi," Kanvar said. "I know you're hurting. Let me help you. You don't have to shield your mind from me, and we're a long way from Stonefountain now. You're safe."

"We're all right now," Aadi murmured, pressing his hand against his chest as if he held something there beneath his shirt. "The sun doesn't hurt me as badly as it does Indumauli, though the salt water really stings our eyes. We hate swimming in the ocean."

"We?" Kanvar said in surprise. "Aadi, are you bound to Indumauli?"

"Something like that," Aadi said. "I hope he catches something to eat quickly. It's been days since we've had food. He couldn't go out and hunt in the river."

"You've bonded? Then you're not a halfblood?" Kanvar said.

Aadi shuddered. "It was dark. You didn't see Indu-mauli's face and head clearly. You didn't see what Khalid did to him when he struck him with the sword. He almost died. The strike almost cut his head clean in half, but Indumauli turned at the last second, and the sword skidded to the side. It cut through his dragonstone." Aadi reached beneath his shirt and pulled out a four-inch sliver of Indu-mauli's dragonstone which he had tied on a string around his neck.

Catching sight of it from over Aadi's shoulder, Kanvar sucked in a surprised breath. "Is Indumauli all right? How badly is he hurt?"

"He's recovering," Aadi said. "He's blind in one eye and his head is kind of lopsided now. Don't tease him about it. It's bothering him. He doesn't want anyone to see how he looks."

"But you look fine," Kanvar said. "You must have bonded with him after he was injured."

"I didn't bond with him," Aadi snapped. "I couldn't bond with him. I'm a halfblood. Believe me, I've tried the whole Choosing Ceremony, Bonding Ceremony thing. It was—" Aadi broke off, choking and shuddering.

"That doesn't make any sense." Denali broke into their conversation. Down lower in Dharanidhar's claw, he was getting a bit wet as the waves sloshed up around him. Dharanidhar had spread his wings out across the water to buoy himself up so he wouldn't have to swim with his back legs. He floated on the ocean, resting and catching his breath. Frost remained on his shoulder, instinctively knowing her fragile wings would not withstand the ocean waves.

"If you aren't bonded and you can't bond," Denali continued. "How come you're talking like you and Indumauli are one person?"

Kanvar had been wondering the same thing, but had not wanted to push Aadi any further. Aadi had been hurt too much already.

"It's the dragonstone," Aadi said. "As long as I'm touching it, Indumauli and I stay linked. It's a bond of sorts, but not a Naga bond. It's just the power of the dragonstone. I doubt it would do that with a normal human, but I am a halfblood. Half, the fountain help me, only half." An edge of bitterness had crept into Aadi's voice.

Dharanidhar let out a deep rumble. *I think I better fly again now before it's too late. I'll have to go slower though and fly low so I can use the air currents coming up off the water to lift me.*

"Right. Go ahead," Kanvar said, gritting his teeth at the stab of pain in Dharanidhar's bad wing as he lurched into the air. "Aadi, will Indumauli be able to follow us below?"

"He can follow," Aadi said. "As long as I have this stone, he can feel me easily." Aadi tucked the shard back beneath his shirt and took a shuddering breath. He leaned back against Kanvar and closed his eyes again. He was so hungry and weak, Kanvar worried that Indumauli wouldn't have the strength to make the ocean crossing.

I'll make it, Indumauli hissed, *we can feel each other, but our physical ailments don't cross over. I'm not as weak as Aadi is. As long as Dharanidhar flies true and I don't get lost down here like I did last time, I won't have any trouble getting to Kundiland.*

I'm not going to get either of us lost, Dharanidhar said.

No, lost isn't going to be the problem, Kanvar agreed. *It'll be the pain.*

Chapter Six

Rajan stood on the cliff ledge above the jungle village and watched the sunrise over the steamy jungle canopy. Amar was away at the palace, getting the young gold dragons settled back into their home. Returning to the palace had been rough for him—so much had happened there. Rajan, who took his job as the king's guardian seriously, had been keeping close watch on Amar wherever he went. Fortunately, Amar had not protested Rajan's constant presence at the edge of his mind. Now, Amar's thoughts were a jumble of unhappy emotions.

After Khalid had returned the singing stones to Stonefountain and the Naga Guard had taken control of the human armies, Captain Vitra and his men had interred Rajahansa's body along with Parmver, Haidar, and Liander and their dragons in the palace burial vault that housed Amar's parents.

Dharanidhar had barely gotten the dragon hunters that had slain Rajahansa out of the palace and hidden in the jungle village before the Naga guardsmen arrived. Amar knelt now in the vault, mourning the dead.

Rajan clenched his fists. There was nothing he could do to quench the king's sorrow. *Bensharie*, Rajan called to Amar's dragon. *I think he's been in there long enough. It's not doing him any good reliving everything that happened leading up to their deaths.*

It was unfortunate that Bensharie was too small to carry both Amar and Rajan on his back. Since Silverwave could not fly, it made it hard for Rajan to stay close to the king when he did crazy things like fly to Varna, or when he needed someone to draw him out of the vault and convince him to return to his wife in the jungle village.

I tried, Bensharie said. *He won't come. I think he just needs time to work this through on his own. He never intended to come back here, but Jaymon and the others need a home. We dragons can't live in the jungle village.*

"I need wings," Rajan grumbled. "I can't get around anywhere without them."

I'm not going to apologize for being serpent, Silverwave responded. She was swimming far out in the open ocean beyond the Maran Colony, keeping lookout. Rajan glanced over at the line of iron spears that rested against the cliff face. Khalid had been quiet for too long, but then wasn't he always quiet? They'd learned from sad experience he seldom worked directly. His vile plans were made up of lies and diversions. But he had the manpower now to launch a decisive retaliation for the defeat of Captain Vitra and the Nagas who had held Kundiland for him. But none had come. No human army. No Nagas.

"What are you up to, Khalid?" Rajan said.

Perhaps he thinks Kundiland isn't worth the trouble, Silverwave said. *He saw into Aadi's mind and knows Qadim and General Chandran are in Varna and Maran. What good would sending an army back here do? No one's here except you, Tana, and Amar.*

That's what worries me. Rajan picked up a spear and spun it in his hands. *He knows the rightful king is here with only Tana and me to protect him. What can we do if he sends the whole army?*

If he sends the humans, you will free their minds. If he sends the Nagas, you will kill them like you did the others.

Rajan let out a bitter laugh. *I'm strong, but not that strong. The most Nagas I think we could take at once is three. He has dozens. If it were me, I'd have come for the king before I wasted manpower on rebuilding Stonefountain.*

He thought Amar was already dead until Aadi showed him otherwise.

Rajan grimaced. *Amar should never have let Aadi go to Stonefountain. It was a stupid mistake.*

He thought it would save Aadi's life.

Rajan set the spear back in place and let his hand drop to the weapons he had secured to his belt. His claws were safely folded and strapped in place so they wouldn't dangle down and cut his legs, but it would only take him a moment to slide his hands inside them and release the straps that held them in place. It would have been nice to have a sword and a crossbow as well, but Amar still carried his sword, and Rajan couldn't exactly fly to Daro to purchase a crossbow.

Do you think Kanvar found Aadi? Rajan asked Silverwave.

It's not like Kanvar to fail at anything he sets his mind to.

I wish Amar would listen to me once in a while. As stupid as it was letting Aadi go to Stonefountain, it's even worse sending Kanvar in after him. Kanvar knows all our plans, everything and everyone involved. It is beyond stupid to risk the entire war, the fate of the world, just to rescue one boy who is most likely dead anyway.

Don't think that way. Amar's sharp voice cut into their conversation. *You sound like Khalid, and we can't let ourselves become like him. We have to care about every single life and do what we can to protect the innocent.*

Rajan rubbed his head. There were disadvantages of keeping such a close watch on the king. It meant that Amar was just as aware of Rajan's thoughts as the other way around. *Forgive me, Your Majesty*, Rajan said.

Rajan. Amar's disapproval continued to wash over Rajan. *I need you to be like a silver serpent not a red dragon. I know you think we need the red dragon's strength right now, but that's not what the world needs, and it's not what I need. What if it were Eleanor trapped in Stonefountain, dying? Would you not do anything, take any risk, to free her?*

Rajan's heart cringed. What if it *were* his own precious daughter trapped in Khalid's clutches? It would still be stupid to risk everything to save her, to put the life of one child before the freedom of the entire world? It would kill him to lose Eleanor but—

Don't think that way, Amar said again. *You love Eleanor and her mother. Love is our greatest strength, Rajan, not our greatest weakness.*

If Eleanor were in Khalid's clutches, I would do whatever you ordered me to do because my life is yours to command, Rajan said. *But my thoughts and beliefs remain my own.* Rajan tore his mind away from the king's and lifted a shield between them.

Someone's coming across the ocean, Silverwave hissed.

Rajan tensed. A black monkey screamed in the jungle below, and a flock of scaly macaws took to the air. *Is it Kanvar?*

No. It's a guardsman and his dragon.

Only one.

Just one. Though it's hard to tell with the way the sun ripples off the water close to the surface. There may be others flying lower.

You should be able to see the Nagas and feel their presence even if you can't see their dragons, Rajan said.

One Naga and his dragon. That's all.

Bensharie, Rajan called. *Someone's coming. I need you to fly out here and take me to the Maran Colony. Whoever it is, I don't want him to get anywhere near the village or the palace.*

Coming, Bensharie answered.

Rajan waited impatiently for Bensharie to land on the ledge. At last, the young gold dragon flapped down to land beside him. Amar rode on Bensharie's back and glanced at Rajan with a troubled look.

"Good, you're here," Rajan said. "You should take the women inside the mountain where they'll be safe while I deal with this."

Amar speared Rajan with a stern look.

"Do you want me to apologize, Your Majesty?"

"No. You're right. I can't tell you how to think and feel. But I'm the king, and I give the orders. You're going to stay here and keep the women safe while I deal with the Naga. He may be an ally."

"He could just as easily be an enemy."

"I gave Taral orders to find people who would support me. We shouldn't be surprised if he's done so."

"You ordered him to have them wait at Stonefountain for your command, not fly out here to Kundiland."

"Rajan, something like this takes delicate negotiation. The guardsmen may need to see for themselves that I'm alive before they believe Taral. Come on, Bensharie, let's go."

Bensharie tried to take off, but Rajan grabbed him around the neck and held his head down so he couldn't fly. "It's my job to protect you, Your Majesty. I can't do that if you keep running off alone."

"Let go of Bensharie," Amar said, a touch of anger easing into his usually calm voice.

"No, you have to listen to me, Amar. Khalid needs to be rid of you. You can't just fly out there to meet whatever assassin he's sent."

"You said Taral was a spy and an assassin too, but my meeting with him went just fine. You can't go on thinking the worst of everyone, Rajan."

"Yes, I can. It's my job, and if I'd known you were going to meet Taral in Varna, I never would have let you go." Rajan held Bensharie tight even though the young dragon strained to break his hold.

"I'm the king. You're supposed to follow my orders not the other way around," Amar said, exasperated.

"I'm your personal guard and I think you should listen to me once in a while," Rajan answered.

How about a compromise, Bensharie said. *You can both go. I'll carry Rajan in my back claws. I've done it before.*

"Then who will protect the women?" Amar said.

Tana's thoughts rose up to them from the village. *Vasanti and I can protect ourselves and Eska and Mani as well. Now stop arguing and go find out what this Naga wants.*

"Fine." Rajan let go of Bensharie and grabbed one of the spears. "Let's go."

"Very well," Amar said. "But don't drive this man away, Rajan. We need all the allies we can get."

Rajan gritted his teeth as Bensharie's talons closed around his shoulders and lifted him into the air. Dangling from the dragon's back claws over the hot jungle was not the most comfortable way to fly. At least Rajan had convinced Amar to let him come. The longer Rajan had waited in Kundiland, the more restless and jumpy he'd become.

Your Majesty, King Amar? A bright Naga voice reached across the jungle to their minds. *Are you here? Are you alive?*

I'm alive, Amar answered. *Wait at the colony near the shore. I'll be there in a few minutes.*

Rajan felt the Naga land in the Maran Colony town square. A while later, Bensharie set Rajan down in the square and landed beside him. Rajan gripped his spear and stared up at the Naga atop his dragon's back. Rajan had seen the man with Captain Vitra in Aesir. *I recognize him*, Rajan told Amar. *He's one of the Elite Guard. One of the men who supported my execution.*

This isn't Aesir, Amar said. *And things have changed since then.*

Things change; people don't. Be cautious, Rajan said.

"You, you're the king?" the man said, looking down in consternation at Amar who had landed on such a small dragon. "But you can't be bound to that . . . youngster. I was told your dragon had died. It was confirmed. They interred the body."

Amar dismounted and motioned for the other man to come down and talk to him.

Rajan gripped his spear and stepped in between the two as the larger dragon set his Naga on the ground. The Naga glared at Rajan. "Get out of the way, renegade."

Amar put a hand on Rajan's shoulder and eased him aside. "I have pardoned Rajan, and he has taken an oath of service to me. Have a care not to insult him. We are family."

Rajan let Amar ease past him, but he followed, positioning himself within spear strike range of the Naga.

The other Naga took a step back. "What proof do I have that you really are King Amar?"

"What proof do we have that you're not an assassin?" Rajan said. "You haven't even bothered to give us your name."

"My name is Lord Jesson." The man made a faint semblance of a bow. "I have sworn service to Lord Theodoric and the king of Stonefountain."

"Which king?" Rajan demanded. "Khalid or Amar." He held the spear in both hands and licked the sticky sweat from his lips. At least Kundiland was warm, not as hot as a volcano, but warmer than Aesir had been.

"That's what I'm trying to figure out," Jesson said. His eyes narrowed a fraction. He kept his mind fully shielded. "Taral told me King Amar was alive, but I had to come see for myself."

The back of Rajan's neck prickled. He blocked Amar's mind from Jesson's with his own shields and stepped back between the two men. "Who's Taral?" Rajan said. "We've never heard of him."

"What—" Amar started to say, but Rajan froze his voice.

"Taral. He is your spy, isn't he?" Jesson said.

Let me go, Amar protested behind Rajan's shield.

Fine, but don't blow Taral's cover, Rajan told him. *This Naga is fishing for information. Don't give it to him or it could be a death sentence for Taral.* He released Amar's mind. Amar backed up a few steps and reached out to Bensharie.

Bensharie came up beside him in a show of support.

"I don't know who Taral is," Rajan said, "but I can assure you this man beside me is King Amar, the rightful king of Stonefountain. My brother has seen him wield the king's sword. There can be no doubt he is the oldest descendant of the royal line. If you wish to serve him, kneel and give him your oath. If not, fly away quickly before I decide you are an enemy and kill you."

"Rajan," Amar said in his calmest most persuasive voice. "It is natural for a man to want to be sure he is making the right choice about whom he swears to serve. My Lord Jesson, I am the king, and I would welcome your service if you wish to give it freely. I will force no man to follow me."

Jesson dropped to one knee. "My King, I swear by Stonefountain to serve you and only you for the rest of my life."

"I'm filled with gratitude to hear that." Amar walked past Rajan and gave Jesson a hand to help him to his feet.

Rajan winced at the touch and kept Amar's mind safely locked behind his own shields.

"Khalid is at Stonefountain," Jesson said. "I don't like the way he's treating people. At first I thought I was serving Devaj, your son, your heir. We all thought you were dead and he was the rightful king. We believed Khalid was merely helping him, but more and more I've come to wonder about that. Khalid is subtly cruel. He hides behind Devaj's smile. Everyone fears to go against him, but I ran away and came here. I had to see if the rumors were true that you were alive."

"I am alive," Amar said.

Jesson turned to look eastward toward Stonefountain. "Then you must do something to stop Khalid." His hand curled around his sword hilt.

Rajan slammed the haft of the spear against Jesson's chest, knocking him away from the king.

"Rajan," Amar snapped as Jesson righted himself and stared at Rajan in wide-eyed shock.

"He was reaching for his sword, Your Majesty. He could have killed you," Rajan said.

"I'm wearing armor." Amar rubbed the glistening golden armor Karishi had fashioned for him.

"Armor that already has too many dents in it," Rajan said.

"Stay back from the king," Rajan ordered Jesson.

Jesson lifted his hand clear of his sword. "I swear I wasn't going to draw it. I was only thinking we must fight Khalid. Surely you have some plan to regain your rightful place on the throne, some plan to destroy him. You can't possibly be content to stay hiding in this vile jungle while the world suffers with his tyranny."

"I—" Amar tried to answer, but once again Rajan froze his voice.

"King Amar has lived peacefully in this jungle for five hundred years," Rajan said. "He is sorry that the humans have been enslaved, but there is nothing he can do about it. They are the ones who came to Kundiland trying to kill him. If they'd stayed in their own land, Khalid never would have been freed from Stonefountain. Believe me, King Amar is sorry for their suffering from the deepest part of his heart, but he has no plans to help them. What can he possibly do? Nothing can stand against Khalid's might and power."

Jesson's eyes grew guarded and his brow wrinkled. "That's not what I heard. There is a rumor that a Maran General and the Varnan dragon hunters are planning an uprising. Surely they're working for you. If you tell me where they are, I can join them. I can help them. You have no singing stones. The humans are powerless against Khalid and the Naga Guard. You need my help and the help of other Naga guardsmen, or your army won't stand a chance against Khalid."

Rajan, please release me, Amar whispered in Rajan's mind.

Rajan released Amar's voice but kept the shields up around his mind. *Stay back, Amar. This man knows only what Khalid must have seen in Aadi's mind. He's a spy trying to get more information. You can't tell him anything.*

You may be wrong, Amar said.

I'm not wrong, but if you want proof, tell him you accept his service and he must return to Stonefountain to await your orders. Tell him nothing else. If he's content with that, you may be right. If he keeps pressing for more, I'm going to tear him to shreds.

Amar cleared his throat. "I-I have no army. Why would I trust the very men who tried to kill me? That makes no sense. If you wish to serve me, Lord Jesson, I command you to return to Stonefountain and wait. If I ever need anything from you, I'll contact your mind and let you know."

"What good could I possibly do you at Stonefountain unless you *are* planning an attack? Why don't you trust me? I can help you. If you don't believe me, if you need proof, I'll open my mind to you, fully, every last bit of it. You need only look to see I am your loyal servant." Lord Jesson dropped the shields from around his mind and held out his hand to Amar.

Amar dropped his own shields and reached for Lord Jesson's mind.

"Wrong answer," Rajan said, keeping Amar's mind firmly locked away from Jesson's where Jesson couldn't tear all of their plans from Amar's thoughts. He handed the spear to Bensharie and slid his hands into his dragon claws, releasing the straps that held them. The sharp metal glinted in the sun as Rajan lunged at Jesson. He whipped Jesson around so one of his claws came to rest across Jesson's throat and the other pressed against his gut.

"Don't kill him!" Amar shouted. "He's sworn himself to my service. Rajan, let him go."

Rajan let out a dark chuckle. "Hear that, Jesson. The king wants me to let you go. He believes your oath. I'd like to believe it too, so I'm going to give you one chance to follow the command he just gave you. Get on your dragon, fly back to Stonefountain, and wait for him to contact you. If you don't do it right now, you're a dead man."

"All right, let me go," Jesson said. "I'll leave now."

Rajan let go of Jesson and stepped back so he could mount his dragon.

Jesson pressed the back of his hand against his bleeding neck and glared at Rajan. He opened his mouth to say something.

Rajan stiffened, ready to finish him.

Jesson thought better of it, climbed on his dragon, and the two lifted off, winging across the water toward Varna.

Rajan grinned at Amar and flicked his wrist so the drops of blood sprayed off the edge of his claw. "That went well. Looks like you have another Naga in your service, Your Majesty."

Amar scowled at him. "I can't imagine he'd willingly serve me at all now. Rajan, I told you not to drive him away."

Rajan snorted and glared after the retreating Naga. "He works for Khalid, and you almost gave away every ally and plan we have. Punish me however you want for disobeying you, Your Majesty, but I will not be sorry for keeping you and the rest of our friends safe."

Amar shook his head and turned away from Rajan. "Come on, Bensharie, let's go home."

Khalid called Rajan every foul name he could think of as Jesson's dragon flew him across the ocean toward Daro. Amar would have fallen for Khalid's deception and told him everything if Rajan hadn't stopped him. Such an irritating and unlikely pair, Khalid couldn't figure out how the two could even stand to keep each other company.

By the Fountain, I wish Rajan were on my side, Khalid fumed. I could use a man like that. I wonder what it would take to bring him over—power, money, women, the chance to kill as indiscriminately as he seems to prefer? Something. But that didn't matter at the moment. What mattered was that Amar had failed to give away information about his army the easy way. That left Khalid no other choice but to drive them out into the open with pure relentless brutality.

Well, if that was what was needed to finish this uprising before it started, that's what Khalid would do. He vowed blood would run in the streets of Daro before another day passed.

Chapter Seven

Dharanidhar glided over the Maran Colony, letting the ocean wind carry him up the river to the cliffs above the jungle village. In the water, Indumauli parted company with Silverwave who had met them out in the ocean and accompanied Indumauli to the mouth of the Black River. Kanvar still held Aadi's limp form tight against his chest. Aadi had slept most of the way across the ocean. Kanvar hurt too much to sleep. Dharanidhar was too weak from pushing himself for so many consecutive days to attempt to shield his pain from Kanvar. Kanvar gritted his teeth as Dharanidhar settled onto the ledge above the jungle village. His massive body took up nearly all the space.

"Kanvar!" Tana reached the top of the stairs, followed closely by Amar. Bensharie flapped up from the village and set a pot of freshly-brewed medicine down beside Dharanidhar before landing.

Dharanidhar's legs gave out, and he slumped to the ground, setting Denali aside, and lowering his neck and head to rest on his foreclaws. Kanvar got the harness unbuckled and handed Aadi down into Amar's outstretched arms.

The movement roused Aadi and he looked around disoriented. "Where am I? I dreamed I was flying."

"You were flying." Amar carried Aadi over and set him on Bensharie's back. "You're home now in Kundiland. Bensharie is going to fly you down to the jungle village. You can rest there and get some food. You're going to be all right."

Bensharie lifted his head, locking Aadi in place. Aadi slumped forward against his neck. *We're home,* he said. *Indumauli, we're home.*

Amar jerked back in surprise at Aadi's clear mental speech. "You've bonded?"

Aadi moaned, covered his face with his arm, and raised his shields.

"Go, Bensharie, take him down to the village," Kanvar said as he slid from Dharanidhar's neck to the ground. His own legs buckled the same as Dharanidhar's had, but Tana caught him.

Bensharie lifted off and winged down to the village.

"He hasn't bonded," Kanvar said as soon as Aadi was out of earshot. "He can't bond."

"But his mind. He spoke as well as any Naga," Amar said.

Kanvar wrapped his arm around Tana and leaned his cheek against her warm black hair. "He's wearing a shard of Indumauli's dragonstone. As long as he's touching it, he's linked with Indumauli. He can hear and speak with his mind. I'm not sure that he has any other powers, but this link with Indumauli, it's enough."

"Enough?" Amar's face was lined with worry.

Tana's strength could no longer hold Kanvar up. He slid out of her grip onto the ground beside Dharanidhar and leaned back against the Great Blue dragon. "Enough to keep him alive, enough to keep him sane, enough that he's no longer hurting. But I'm curious." Kanvar looked over at Denali and Frost. "Denali, what did you do with the Great White dragonstone we brought with us from the North?"

Denali frowned and rested his hand on Frost's back. The dragonstone was her father's and Denali did not like to talk about it around her. "It's in my chamber at the palace. Come on Frost." Denali led Frost to the stairs, and the two started down to the village.

"Kanvar." Tana knelt in front of him and brushed worried fingers down his cheek. "Dharanidhar's not moving. Tell him he has to drink the medicine before he falls asleep."

Dhar, wake up, Kanvar coaxed.

Dharanidhar groaned and shifted then settled back to sleep.

Kanvar shook his head. "He's seldom flown so far so quickly since he was injured." At least with Dharanidhar asleep, Kanvar couldn't feel the pain.

"Hey!" Tana shouted, slapping Dharanidhar's foreleg. *"Wake up you useless lizard!"*

Dharanidhar roused and blinked down at her through Kivi's eyes. *What do you want, little green wyrmling?* He grumbled.

Tana pointed to the black pot nearly as large as she was that steamed next to Dharanidhar's foreclaw. "Drink your medicine before I have Vasanti come up here and force it down your gullet."

Dharanidhar mumbled a thank you and gulped down the liquid. Kanvar winced and swallowed, hating the bitter flavor of the medicine. It didn't sit well on Dharanidhar's empty stomach.

Kivi hissed. Kanvar figured he should get up and find some food for the little serpent, but he couldn't move, much less walk down the stairs, so he waited until Bensharie returned to the ledge, and Tana and Amar helped him up onto Bensharie's back. A few minutes later, Bensharie settled onto the platform next to Tana's old hut. Mani and Eska met him there and helped Kanvar down from Bensharie's back.

Thank you, Bensharie, Kanvar said. *Good thing you're small enough to fit down through the canopy.*

I wasn't at first. Elkatran and I had to clear a path through several trees to give us clear passage so we could evacuate the villagers. Not the easiest thing to do, but we did it. Bensharie drew himself up, proud of their accomplishment.

Will you go to the palace and get the Great White dragonstone for me? Kanvar asked Bensharie. Bensharie said he would and flew off.

Kanvar let the women lead him inside and ease him down on the sleeping mat.

Aadi was sitting against a wall of the hut where the daylight couldn't reach him. Eska handed him a bowl of poi and plate of minced mushrooms. "Eat, dear. When you're a little stronger you'll have fish and bread as well. But start with this. You're far too thin. Don't they feed children at all in Stonefountain?"

Aadi shook his head. "There was food at the palace. I couldn't eat it. I had no reason to live."

"You have reason now," Kanvar said. "Eat, so Indumauli doesn't feel your hunger."

Aadi nodded and began to nibble at the food.

Tana and Amar entered the hut, and Kanvar wished vaguely that they had put Aadi somewhere else so he and Tana could be alone. The last time they'd seen each other they'd talked only briefly. A few sentences was all. He'd told her he loved her. He'd kissed her, but Tana may have thought that was only for show so Kanvar could give her the decanter with Bensharie's blood in it and tell her how to use it to save Amar. That tense moment had passed quickly between them, and Kanvar had not seen her since.

Amar went over to speak quietly with Aadi, and Tana sat down beside Kanvar, pressing a bowl of poi into his good hand. "You should eat too."

Kanvar glanced down at the bowl and let a smile curl his lips. "I don't know. You could be trying to poison me. That medicine tasted sour enough to be poison."

Tana laughed, remembering when Kanvar had first come to the village and truly believed Tana had put poison in the food she offered him. "I assure you my poi is as sweet as ever. It will clear the taste of the poison—I mean *medicine*—from your tongue."

Kanvar chuckled, set the bowl in his lap, and shoveled a few spoonfuls of the soothing poi into his mouth.

"I haven't seen you for so long," Tana said. "And whenever you are around we only get to spend a few moments together. It's not fair."

Kanvar swallowed and reached for Tana's hand with his crippled left thumb and fingers. She took his left hand without hesitating. Her fingers were warm and soft against his. "I'm sorry. I didn't mean to get carried off by Khalid to Stonefountain. Believe me, I would much rather have been here with you."

Tana smiled, her green eyes sparkling, the smooth gray skin of her face glowing in the light from the window. "When you return to Stonefountain to fight Khalid, I am going with you. There's nothing you can say or do to stop me."

Kanvar set the bowl of poi aside. Despite feeling uncomfortable with his father and Eska in the room, he ran his fingers along Tana's braided hair, leaned forward, and kissed her. It was a warmer kiss than the one they'd shared on the beach in the rain. Her lips were soft, and impressions of jungle greenery and bright flowers washed over him from her mind. She pulled away after a moment with a sigh and glanced over Kanvar's shoulder at the other people in the room.

"This may not be the best time," she whispered.

"I know." Kanvar kissed her again. "I just wanted to make sure you knew I meant what I said before. I love you, Tana."

Tana laughed softly. "I love you too." She moved away from him and stood. "Now finish that bowl while I go fetch some more substantial food. A Great Blue dragon needs meat, not poi, to survive."

"I won't argue with that," Kanvar said. "But, Tana, don't take too long. Since Dharanidhar is going to have to rest here for a while before he can fly again, I want to spend every minute with you that I can."

Tana smiled and let herself out of the hut.

Behind Kanvar, Amar cleared his throat. "You're a little young to be . . . getting involved with a woman. I didn't marry my first wife until I was—"

Kanvar twisted around to face his father, Eska, and Aadi. "What, two hundred years old or something? Pardon me if I don't think I'll live that long. We're going to Stonefountain to fight Khalid. He probably has ten thousand human soldiers plus all the Naga guardsmen. There are only seven of us: You, me, Rajan, Tana, Theodoric, LaShawn, and Karishi, and whatever stray group of humans Kumar Raza, General Chandran, and Qadim can coble together. I'm not going to throw myself against such an unbeatable foe without first making sure the people I love know how I feel about them."

"You left out Denali and me," Aadi said.

"You are not going to Stonefountain," Kanvar said. "I just risked everything to bring you back from there. Besides, someone needs to stay and defend Kundiland."

Denali burst into the room. He had the iron helmet clutched in his hand instead of on his head and Frost on his heels. "We are to going to Stonefountain, and there's nothing you can do to stop us. You're not that much older than we are, Kanvar. Aadi and I are not children, and we know how to fight."

"I don't question your ability to fight," Kanvar said. "I worry about the strength of your minds."

Denali tossed the helmet on the floor beside Kanvar. It landed with a loud thud and rolled up against Kanvar's legs. "I'll wear it if I have to." Denali jerked the hunting knife from its sheath at his waist. "But with my connection to Frost or without it, I will fight against Khalid."

Amar frowned in disapproval, and Kanvar sensed Amar was having second thoughts about the whole plan. He didn't want anyone he cared about to go to Stonefountain where they could not possibly win without the singing stones.

Kanvar stood. The medicine had started to work, and strength was returning to him. "Father, I think there may be something that can replace the power of the singing stones, something even better if you're willing to try it."

Keeping his mind guarded against false hope, Amar got to his feet. "What?"

Bensharie landed on the platform outside. Kanvar limped out of the hut and accepted the Great White dragonstone from him. Returning to his father, he held up the stone. "You've seen what a single shard of Indumauli's dragonstone has done for Aadi. And I used this white stone to break through the block in Kumar Raza's mind that neither you nor Parmver with all your combined strength and experience could penetrate. I did something similar with a Great Red dragonstone to heal Rajan's mind as well. The dragonstones have power. It is the stones that give the Great dragons the ability to speak. In fact, it may be that the Naga power itself stems from our ability to bond with the Great dragons and tap into the power of their stones. But let's do a little experiment. Denali—"

Kanvar limped over to Denali and pressed the Great White dragonstone into Denali's free hand. "Talk to me, Denali, with your mind. Talk to Frost."

Denali's eyes widened as the stone in his hand, the dead stone that had been dark and empty a moment before, lit deep in its center with a pale white light. Frost let out a surprised squawk and fluttered around the room in excitement.

Kanvar? Denali's mind spoke clear and true into Kanvar's.

Kanvar dropped the personal shields around his mind. Denali gasped. *I can see everything . . . everything you are thinking, your memories.* Kanvar lifted the shields back in place so his mind wouldn't overwhelm Denali's.

Aadi frowned. "Do you think that will work for humans as well?" His words were laced with bitterness, and Kanvar wondered if Aadi would ever come to terms with the fact that he was not a Naga.

"We can find out," Kanvar said, handing the stone to Eska. But even with Amar coaching her on how to speak with her mind, Eska could not do it.

"You see, Aadi," Kanvar said. "You are much more than human. You have something that human men will never have, a link with Indumauli, strong and powerful. You are not alone now, and you need never be."

Aadi pressed his hand against the shard beneath his shirt and nodded.

"Unless Frost protests the use of her father's stone," Kanvar said to Denali, "I think you should wear it around your neck as well. With it, I don't think you'll need that helmet. Aadi can teach you everything about controlling your mind that Parmver taught him."

"Then we can both go with you to Stonefountain?" Denali said hopefully.

Amar shook his head. "This is nice for Aadi and Denali, but I can't see how it will help us defeat Khalid."

Kanvar grinned. "That's because you're not seeing the full picture yet." *Rajan*, he called out with his mind. *Will you join us for a moment?*

Chapter Eight

Rajan strode into the room, his hands resting lightly on the dragon claws hooked to his belt. A dark look passed between Rajan and Amar. Amar's jaw tightened and he turned away. Watching the exchange, Kanvar grew concerned. He did not like to see animosity between Rajan and Amar. Something must have happened between them that would need to be dealt with.

"What is it, Kanvar?" Rajan asked. He fidgeted as if uncomfortable being in the same hut with Amar.

Kanvar glanced back and forth between the two men. "Is there a problem?"

Rajan's eyes flashed. Amar shook his head, but would not make eye contact with Kanvar or Rajan.

"It looks like a problem to me," Kanvar said. "What happened?"

"Nothing much," Amar said. "One of the Naga guards-men came here to swear himself to my service, but Rajan tried to kill him. The man said and did nothing wrong, but Rajan bound my tongue so I couldn't speak to him and drove him away."

"He was a spy," Rajan said, "trying to get information about our plans. If I had not stopped His Majesty, every advantage we have in secrecy would have been lost."

"He wasn't a spy." Amar got to his feet and glared at Rajan.

Rajan opened his mouth to argue back, but Aadi spoke up. "Which guardsman?"

"Lord Jesson," Amar said. "He swore himself to my service."

Aadi sucked in a sharp breath. "Lord Jesson would never do that and mean it. He's head of the Elite Guard, Khalid's right-hand man. He executed two of his own men as traitors just for thinking they might have supported you if you had lived."

Amar's eyes widened. Rajan rolled his shoulders and stroked his dragon claws but refrained from gloating ver-bally. "I'm sorry, Amar." He bowed to the king and started to leave the hut.

"Wait," Kanvar said. "That's not why I called you."

Rajan turned back. "I'm not interested in any more arguments. If you don't approve of what I've done, I really don't care."

Kanvar clenched his right hand into a fist. What he was about to suggest could very well spark even more disagreement between Amar and Rajan. And yet what choice did he have? They desperately needed something to replace the singing stones he'd failed to get.

"Rajan." Kanvar drew himself up to his full height and straightened his shoulders. "I need you to summon Erebus's dragonstone." Erebus the Devourer was the Great Red volcanic dragon Rajan had once been bound to.

Rajan's hands tightened on his claws in surprise, and he cut himself. He jerked his hand up and stared at the blood that trickled down his fingers.

"No, Kanvar," Amar said. "Rajan, don't do it. You're having a hard enough time controlling yourself as it is."

"I'm not having a hard time controlling myself," Rajan said. "It's you I can't control."

"You're not supposed to be controlling me. You're supposed to be following my orders," Amar said.

"When I agreed to live my life in your service, I did not know you would be so reckless and . . . idiotic." Rajan licked the blood from his fingers and glared at Amar.

Kanvar wished Kumar Raza were present. It seemed foolish to have left these two men to work with each other. Kanvar grabbed his flask of dragon saliva from his belt, dumped some into his hand, and spread the saliva across the cuts Rajan had inadvertently given himself.

"Erebus is dead," Kanvar said to both men. "His presence and memories do not exist in the dragonstone. Using

Erebus's stone cannot call his spirit back. I don't think there is any danger it will corrupt Rajan, and there is the slight chance it will make him powerful enough he can engage the minds of more than one Naga guardsman at a time. Rajan, I am certain you are connected enough to that dragonstone to be able to summon it. Please do it now."

Rajan huffed. "Unfortunately, I don't take orders from you, Kanvar. Your Majesty, may I please summon the stone and test Kanvar's theory?"

Amar frowned.

"Father," Kanvar said. "This could be the answer to our problems."

Tana pushed her way through the door of the hut, carrying a plate of roasted black monkey legs. "Here you go, Kanvar." She froze, sensing the tension in the hut. "Oh, come on. I'm not that bad of a cook."

Kanvar grinned and took the plate from her. "I'm hungry enough it wouldn't matter how you cooked. Thank you, Tana." He sat down on the mat and started stuffing the spicy meat into his mouth. There really wasn't much more he could say. Getting Erebus's stone was just the beginning. There were other stones to be gathered that could be even harder for Amar to deal with.

Amar sighed and rubbed his head. "You're sure it won't . . . hurt you?" he asked Rajan.

Rajan frowned. "My link to Erebus is gone. Sharing Erebus's mind and body was startlingly intoxicating. There is no way I can explain it so you'll understand the all-consuming power I once controlled. But I'll never share Erebus's spirit again."

"You didn't control Erebus," Amar said softly. "Erebus controlled you. I've discussed it with Silverwave. She was there. She saw how you interacted with the red dragon. You had no will of your own."

"It doesn't matter who was in control; Erebus is dead," Rajan said. "What could it hurt to summon the stone? Either it will work the way Kanvar is hoping it will, or it will do nothing but look pretty on a shelf in my hut. I don't see any risk in calling it other than my own discomfort at remembering the things I used to do, and believe me, I don't need the stone to remember and regret that part of my life."

Amar relented. "I leave the choice to you, Rajan. I just hope whatever power you may gain from the stone does not cause you to break your oaths to me and lure you back to the person you were before Erebus died."

Kanvar felt Rajan's thoughts drift to the love he felt for his wife, Dove, and their little daughter, Eleanor. "Nothing could make me go back to being what I was," Rajan said.

Embarrassed at sensing Rajan's intimate thoughts, Kanvar held out the plate of monkey legs to Aadi. "These are good. Want some?"

Aadi shook his head.

Tana sat down next to Kanvar and clasped his left hand.

Rajan turned away from them, cupped his hands in front of him, and focused his mind. A few quiet moments later, Erebus's stone appeared in his grasp. Rajan turned back to face Kanvar, Amar, and Tana. Uncomfortable seeing such Naga powers in use, Eska excused herself and left the hut.

Aadi leaned forward as Rajan directed his thoughts into the stone. Denali and Frost moved closer to watch. A faint red light began to glow in the stone. Then the power exploded, resonating between the stone, Rajan's mind, and Silverwave. It sent out a shock wave that shattered Kanvar's shields and burned through his mind.

Rajan gasped and brought the power quickly back under control before he hurt anyone. "Sorry about that," he said, pulling his mind back from the stone, which fell dark once more. "Yes, Kanvar. I think you're right. There is a lot of potential here. This just might even the odds a bit between us and the other Nagas." Rajan stared down at the large red jewel he held with both hands. "The problem is, while I'm holding this, I can't use my other weapons."

Having eaten his fill, Kanvar set the plate aside and wrapped his good arm around Tana's shoulders. "I've been thinking about that. It's too heavy to wear on a string around your neck like Aadi's, but it would look very nice set into a breastplate of red dragonscale armor like Kumar Raza's. Raza would never give his armor up, of course, but there is a lesser red volcanic dragon lurking near here. Tana and I ran into it not that long ago. If you were to grab a couple of spears and have Bensharie show you how Kumar Raza hunts the red dragons, I think you could fashion yourself a handsome bit of armor, even better than Kumar Raza's, once you've set that dragonstone into it."

Rajan grinned. "I like you, Kanvar. It's a pleasure to work with you." *Bensharie*, he called, striding from the hut. *Come show me how my brother defeated Erebus.*

"Well, I guess we have our weapon against the Naga Guardsmen now," Amar said. He still felt uncomfortable with so much power in Rajan's hands, but he could see that Kanvar was right. Here was a weapon they could use.

Kanvar swallowed a lump in his throat. That had been the easy one. "Tana," he said, drawing her closer against him. "I don't want you to be angry with me, but I think you could be equally as powerful, or at least a good deal stronger than you are now, if you wielded Mahanth's dragonstone."

"What?" Tana pulled away from him, and Vasanti's roar rattled the hut.

Kanvar winced. He hadn't realized Vasanti was that close by. "Tana, Tana, listen. I know you told me not to take Mahanth's dragonstone, that it would bring a curse down upon the village that would destroy it. And you were right. Look around you; the village is deserted. As a direct result of my actions, General Chandran brought the human armies here, which forced the abandonment of your home. But whether you're comfortable using the stone against

Khalid or not, I think you should at least have Amar help you summon it back here so it can be returned to Mahanth's burial mound. Then maybe the curse will be broken, and your people will be able to return to their homes."

Tana put her hands on her hips. "My people will never be safe here while Khalid rules at Stonefountain. Returning Mahanth's stone will not undo what you've done."

"No, but destroying Khalid will," Kanvar said, holding his hand out to Tana. "I need you to help us fight, Tana. We need you to be as powerful as you possibly can be. Vaanti was Mahanth's mate; she's certain to be attuned to Mahanth's dragonstone. In your hands, that stone can help break this curse."

Tana stilled and closed her eyes, having a private conversation with Vasanti. Tears streaked Tana's cheeks as she opened her eyes and walked over to Amar. "Vasanti agrees. You can use her memories of Mahanth to find his dragonstone and bring it home."

"Are you sure," Amar said, taking her hands gently in his own.

Tana nodded. "Kanvar's right. We need to do this."

It took a while for Amar to gather enough connection from Tana and Vasanti's minds to summon the dragonstone, but he did it at last. The green jewel appeared in Tana's hands, and she pressed it against her chest. As she did, Amar manipulated her armor so the stone became a part of it. A soft green light filled the hut. Tana sucked in a breath and stroked the stone, amazed at the power. It was not the hot fire of the red dragonstone that had shattered Kanvar's shields and burned across his mind. The green dragonstone emanated the patient power of growing things— roots delving ever deeper for moisture and nutrients, branches reaching strong arms ever higher to embrace the sunlight, the power of throbbing vibrant life that filled the jungle.

"It's beautiful," Tana said.

Kanvar kissed her forehead. "As are you." He turned to face his father. This last would be the hardest.

"Bensharie is young," Kanvar said. "His heart is big, but his stone is small. Father."

Understanding hit Amar as if Kanvar had reached out and shoved him. He stumbled back against the hut wall, his hand pressed to his heart. "No, Kanvar. I can't."

"Father, try to think of the five hundred years you and Rajahansa lived together as friends. He broke at the end, swayed by Khalid's lies, but there is no reason to focus all your memories on that. Try to re-live all the good times you had together. He was ever your friend, always a good companion. Your bond was pure and wholesome once, and Rajahansa's dragonstone could be used for good again in your hands."

Amar shook his head, wordlessly.

"Father, you need to do this."

Amar let out a cry of despair and retreated from the hut, calling for Bensharie.

Chapter Nine

Bensharie landed on the platform outside the hut. Amar strode over to him and leaned against the young dragon's chest. Neither said anything for a long moment. "Let's get out of here," Amar said finally.

Kanvar had not come out after him, but Amar did not want to talk to anyone in the village. Certainly not Kanvar or Rajan, not even his wife, Mani. Things had been a bit strained between the two of them since . . . since when? He tried to think. Since they came to the village? Since Rajahansa was killed? Or before that. Since Haidar and Liander had abused her in the palace? Or even farther back. Since she found out Amar was a Naga and tried to kill him? That had been a breaking point, one he'd worked hard to mend since he'd brought her to live with him in Kundiland. He'd promised her she'd be safe and happy at the palace. That had not turned out to be true. At least she was not the only woman here now. Thank the fountain, Tana and Eska kept her company. Amar doubted he was much good for companionship at the moment. For her part, Mani had tried hard to rebuild their relationship. If there was a breach, it came from Amar's heart.

You're afraid to let yourself love, Bensharie said as he took flight with Amar on his back, *because of Rajahansa. You fight with Rajan. You fight with Kanvar. You are gentle with the ladies, but your heart is cold, even with your wife.*

She senses it, Amar said.

Bensharie lifted above the canopy and hovered in the sunlight. The throb of insects, the call of monkeys and birds, and the hiss of lesser dragons gave life to the towering trees beneath them. The Black River twisted its way toward the coast like a snake through the greenery. *Have you been fighting with Mani too?* Bensharie asked. He always kept himself fully shielded from Amar when he spent time with his wife.

Amar winced. *We've been having a disagreement.*

About?

She does not want me to go to Stonefountain. She doesn't want me to fight Khalid. She's begging me to flee to Navgarod and go into hiding there. The hot sun beat against his armor, drenching him in sweat. His robes were so much more comfortable. Perhaps he should go back to the palace and get some.

Bensharie flapped his wings and headed inland toward the palace. *She mirrors your own doubts and desires. You're afraid we can't win, and you'll be responsible for the deaths of everyone you love.*

You know my heart better than anyone, Bensharie. Amar leaned his face against Bensharie's hot neck. The smell of molten gold enfolded him.

That's why I know we're not going to the palace just to gather some better clothing.

Amar closed his eyes and let the ground speed by below him as Bensharie flew as smooth as a wisp of cloud on the wind. *Do you think we can defeat Khalid, Bensharie?*

Of course we can. Good always triumphs over evil.

Only in story books. Amar had already failed to defeat Khalid in the battle that had mattered most to him. Khalid had won Rajahansa's heart and mind.

The tales of battle between good and evil exist in books because those are the stories that are important enough to write down. The scribes preserved the stories of the ancient heroes of Stonefountain because they knew someday their descendants would have to fight their own battles and would need to know that they can win even when things seem the most hopeless. Bensharie glided down to land on the golden sunburst in the palace's central hall. Amar remained seated on his back.

Bensharie snorted and headed deeper into the palace. When the hall he followed ended against the cliff face, he ascended a curved staircase up to the next level and the next until he came into a large semi-circular chamber at the top. There was an arched window in the chamber, big enough even Ceiron could have fit through, but it was closed, sealed with a wall of pure gold, leaving the chamber devoid of light.

Amar remained unmoving on Bensharie's back. Bensharie lit a torch and moved to stand in front of another great arch opposite the window, this one etched into the stone of the mountain itself.

Well, Bensharie said, *do you want me to come in with you this time?*

It won't make any difference. They'll still be dead.

I can get the dragonstone, Amar. You don't have to do it. Bensharie stepped up to the arch and placed his foreclaw on the stone.

Who says I've come for Rajahansa's dragonstone. I told Kanvar no.

Your voice said no. Your heart said yes, because you have a choice of whether you fight or you run, and you've already chosen, just like you told Taral. You will face Khalid, whatever the cost.

Would fleeing to Navgarod be such a bad thing? Amar slid off Bensharie's back but could not bring himself to take the torch from his claw.

You could never leave your oldest son in Khalid's clutches and the humans cruelly enslaved.

Amar slumped against the rock door. His eyes stung and he found it hard to speak aloud, but he did so anyway, because what needed to be said should be spoken out loud at least once. "The only way to free Devaj from Khalid is to kill him. I don't want to have to kill my own son. I don't want Devaj to die."

Perhaps there's some other way.

"You know there's not. Devaj has to die, and everyone who goes with me to Stonefountain to accomplish that task will likely die as well." Amar's heartbeat thundered in his ears. There, he'd said it, what he'd wanted to say all along, every time General Chandran, Rajan, and Kumar Raza talked of their plans to defeat Khalid. None of them had spoken the obvious truth—we're going to kill Devaj. We're going to destroy your son, your heir, the child you waited five hundred years to father. Even Kanvar was still denying the truth, seeking ways to become powerful enough to kill his own brother.

Amar let out a wrenching sob. "I can't, Bensharie. I can't fight Devaj. I can't kill him. If it must be done, can't it be done without me? Why did Khalid have to take Devaj when I was willing to give my own life instead? Why? Why?" He slammed his fists against the uncaring stone, bruising his hands and tearing his skin.

Bensharie wrapped a foreclaw around Amar and drew him back against his chest so he couldn't hurt himself more by battering at the rock face. *I will tell Kanvar that he and the others must go to Stonefountain without you. You and I will stay here with the women. You are right. It is too much to ask you to kill your own son.*

Amar breathed heavily but couldn't seem to get enough air into his lungs. He felt Bensharie's mind make contact with Kanvar's but could not hear what the two said to each other. At last Bensharie pulled away and turned his thoughts to Amar.

Kanvar says he has a plan to defeat Khalid and save Devaj both. I think it might just work, but he needs you to be there. A

Naga named Fistas met Kanvar in Stonefountain. He covered Kanvar's escape with Aadi and Indumauli. Fistas sent you a message that Taral has done his job. The guardsmen willing to fight against Khalid are waiting there for you to lead them.

"Kanvar thinks he has a way to save Devaj?" The faintest sliver of hope lit in Amar's heart, but he was too afraid of being disappointed to let it grow into a warm flame.

He seems pretty certain. You left before he could tell you the rest of his plan. He says he and Dharanidhar know where Akshara was laid to rest.

"Akshara?"

Akshara was as old as Ceiron when he died. His stone is giant, ancient, and powerful. Wielded by Kanvar and Dharanidhar, the Great Blue Liberator's dragonstone might just be enough to overpower Khalid. Bensharie let go of Amar and put the torch into his hand. *Your job will not be to fight Khalid, it will be to rally the Naga Guardsmen to your side and stop Khalid's human soldiers from massacring General Chandran's army. Kanvar and the others know you well enough. They don't want you to kill anyone; they want you to save thousands of lives. The stronger you are, the more people you can save. That's why you need to get Rajahansa's dragonstone.*

Amar swallowed. He wanted to believe Bensharie was right. Fighting back his fear and misgivings, he pressed his free hand against the rock face and manipulated the stone so a human-sized door swung open, revealing the burial vault beyond. "Wait here," he told Bensharie.

Bensharie bowed and moved away from the door.

Amar stepped inside and closed the stone behind him. The flame of his torch lit the long chamber. To his left, the Naga dead had been laid to rest in marble coffins. Unlike the rest of the palace that was overlaid with gold, there was no gold in the burial vault. The coffins were white as bleached bones, the stone as cold and dead as the loved ones laid inside. The first to die had been Parmver's oldest son, betrayed by a human he thought was his friend. Amar had not yet been born when Ettan had died. He had not known Ettan, still Amar kissed his own hand and rested it for a moment on the cold stone of Ettan's coffin before moving on to the next two.

Though Amar had been young when his parents were killed by Naga hunters, he was old enough to remember them. His father had a ready wit and a bright smile. Amar had never seen him sad or angry. His mother had been gentle and soft spoken. Neither of his parents had seen the hunters tracking them or imagined the ambush that had caused their deaths. Amar kissed his hand once more and rested it in turn on each coffin, in honor to the dead. What his life would have been like had they lived, he would never know.

Two elegantly carved coffins lay beyond those of his parents: Amar's human wives. He'd loved each in turn, even as she aged and left him in death. His children and grandchildren by these women had been buried in the jungle as was the villagers' custom. But Amar had laid these two beautiful women to rest beside his parents. His love for them would never grow dim. To each of these he bent and kissed the smooth stone with his lips. "I love you," he whispered.

Next lay Parmver. The dear old man had given his life to buy Amar's freedom. Amar knew that if Parmver were standing in front of him now, he would tell Amar not to mourn for him. He'd lived a good long life and died a noble death. He'd always told Amar to live a life of no regrets. Certainly Parmver had lived his life that way. It had been Parmver who had raised and trained Amar after his parents' deaths. The world felt like a cold and empty place with Parmver gone. Amar knelt and bowed his head beside Parmver's coffin for a long time before rising, saluting the dead with a kiss of his hand, and moving on.

Haidar and Liander had been laid to rest on the far side of Parmver. Parmver's two sons had built the golden palace Amar had played in as a child and grown to adulthood in. They were so much older than Amar they had spent scarce time with him as he grew. He had often wondered at their aloofness, but Parmver waved it away as simply their nature. Yet, on rare unguarded moments, Amar could have sworn he felt jealously from their minds. Amar was the son of the king, heir to the throne of Stonefountain, a royal child, and Parmver doted on him. Amar had never been sure if Haidar and Liander were jealous of their father's affection for Amar, or jealous of Amar's crown. He wondered what Khalid had promised them in return for their aid in chaining Amar and keeping him prisoner. Amar shook his head and turned away from their coffins with no token of respect.

Across from the human coffins was a row of stone vaults. The gold dragons who had been laid to rest here in the mountain, were too big to fit into a coffin, so the vaults had been constructed around their bodies. The vault of each dragon stood roughly across from its fallen Naga. Only the vault on the end stood alone. Amar stared at it for a long time. The Naga guardsmen who had entombed Rajahansa had done so with care worthy of a king. The marble was carved with a picture of the palace at Stonefountain where a pride of gold dragons bowed in homage to the Great Gold Dragon King. The image of Rajahansa at the top with wings spread in glory was accented by a dazzling sunburst behind it.

If Lord Theodoric and his Naga Guard had arrived only a few hours sooner, Rajahansa would still be alive. The care with which the guardsmen had laid Rajahansa to rest led Amar to believe in the innate goodness of their hearts. Khalid could not have corrupted so many noble men. Amar's interaction with Lord Taral had confirmed that. And now Kanvar had brought word that Taral had made contact with others. As much as Amar did not want to go to Stonefountain, as much as his wife begged him not to, Amar felt a responsibility to these men. He was supposed to be their king. They expected him to lead them.

"I've never really had to be a king before," he said so softly he could barely hear his own voice. "Parmver, I don't know how to lead these men."

Listen to your heart, an even softer voice tugged at the edge of his mind.

Amar's hand tightened on the torch, and he looked around the chamber but saw no one. *Bensharie, did you say something?*

Bensharie turned his attention to Amar. *No, not really. I was just reciting some poetry. Maybe you overheard one of the lines.*

Amar shook his head.

You're taking a long time. Just get the dragonstone, Bensharie nudged him.

Don't push me, Bensharie. I'm doing this as fast as I can. Amar crossed the chamber and laid a hand on Rajahansa's vault.

A whisper of indecipherable voices brushed Amar's consciousness. He jerked his hand back in surprise and dropped the torch. It guttered and went out. The sudden darkness was overpowering. Amar's heart beat loud, and a drumbeat from within the mountain answered. Amar froze. With his visual perception gone, his sense of hearing increased, but the drums were not a living sound. He felt them in his mind like a heartbeat, slow and solemn, resonating from the mountain itself. As Amar turned his mind toward the sound, other drums joined in, thumping a faster counterbeat. The drumbeat of the rocks remained steady while the other drums pattered like the heartbeats of unnumbered trees, living, growing, reaching for the sunlight. In a wash of vibrant sound, the voices returned, chanting, spinning out pictures in Amar's mind of all the living creatures of the jungle. The words of the chant spoke of life and death and life beyond. This was the heart of the jungle. This was eternity.

A sunburst of gold flecks pulsed to life in the rock wall at the far back of the chamber. Amar stumbled toward it. The specks danced with the rhythm of the drums and the chant. Amar pressed his hand against the sunburst, and the song drove inside him, rattling his bones with its intensity. He tried to pull his hand away, but found he could not.

Follow your heart, Parmver's voice spoke into his mind. But it couldn't be. Parmver was dead. Amar glanced over his shoulder into the darkness where the coffins lay.

Death is a fool's word for the door to eternity, Parmver's voice rose above the chant as it grew louder. *Come, Amar. Join us for a moment.*

The rock face sprang open, revealing a round chamber beyond. Gold specks in the walls twinkled like a million stars in the nighttime sky. Water dripped as a misty rain from the walls and ceiling and gathered in a pool in the center of the floor. A green glow rose up from the bottomless pool. The song of the jungle, the drums and the voices, filled Amar with unspeakable joy and sorrow.

A swirl of pale mist rose from the pool and took on Parmver's visage. *Welcome to the Hall of your Ancestors*, Parmver said.

Amar fell to his knees. "Aren't my ancestors dwelling in Stonefountain?"

Those that have died here, reside here, Parmver said. *Though there are more dragon spirits in this place than human or Naga spirits.*

"Then my parents . . . ?"

Yes, Parmver said while the song of the jungle continued unabated.

"My wives?"

Would you like to speak with them?

Amar bowed his head. "I do not know what I would say beyond what I've said a thousand times. I love them. They should know that already."

All those you care about do know that you love them, all but one. Parmver folded his ghostly arms across his chest. *You and Rajahansa have unfinished business.*

A pain stabbed Amar's heart. "He's here?"

Of course.

Amar pressed his hand to his chest. "I can't talk to him, Parmver. I can't. There's nothing to say."

Parmver's eyes flashed. *There is much that needs to be said. Call him, Amar. Summon his spirit to face you. His anger and regret trouble our song.*

"I can't change that. I can't undo what he's done." Amar told himself to get up and leave the chamber, but his body refused to move.

Dragonbound IX

You must face him, if not for his sake or our sakes, then for your own. Parmver's spirit dissipated into wisps of fog that settled into the pool and vanished.

Amar shivered and the tone of the chant changed into a deeper thrum, the drums pounding and the female voices going silent. The falling water soaked his hair and slid down his neck to wet his chest and arms beneath his armor. The pool glowed a faint green, the walls glittered gold. Green and gold, the colors of life in the jungle. Amar stared into the empty pool for a long time before easing his hand down into the water. Ghostly faces flashed across the surface, all the dead he had known and loved in life. They appeared before him only for a moment before flitting away. But Rajahansa did not come.

Rajahansa's anger and regret, Amar thought, can they be greater than my own? Amar clenched his fist in the water. *Rajahansa*, he cried out with his mind, reaching for the essence he knew as Rajahansa, for the sense of being that had for so long been part of his own.

The glow at the heart of the pool changed from green to gold. A swirl of gold mist lifted from the water as Parmver had done, but Rajahansa's spirit was far bigger than Parmver's. Rajahansa spread his wings and they filled the chamber and went out beyond into the rocks. He roared, and the song of the jungle fell silent.

From his knees, Amar stared up into Rajahansa's ravaged face. "You betrayed me," Amar said. "You tortured my mind and chained me in my own hall. You destroyed Aadi and murdered Parmver. I see no rest for your soul. You willfully did these things. Do not try to tell me that Khalid controlled you and you had no free will of your own. You cannot hide your mind or heart from me."

Rajahansa roared again. His eyes were aflame with fury. *You are not innocent in this, Amar. Do not try to claim that you weren't the architect behind bringing the dragon hunters to the palace to slay me.*

"I did what had to be done to stop you from freeing Khalid from Stonefountain."

The fire died from Rajahansa's eyes. *You failed and so did I. Khalid used us both.* Rajahansa shook his head as if he could clear his mind of Khalid's influence. *I should not have listened to him. He lied to me from the beginning, and I believed him. I trusted him. If only I had not listened to him the first time he reached his mind out to me. But I thought I was strong, and he could never hurt me. I listened to him, just a little, then a little more. Each time, though I argued with him, what he said made more and more sense. In the end, all I could hear were his lies. You were not there when I killed Parmver. I swear to you, if you had been linked with my mind, you would have known how hard I tried to fight him. I tried to resist, but he'd taken too much control by then, and you weren't there to help me. I'd already driven you away. I will never be free of the torment killing Parmver has brought me.*

Rajahansa's spirit dissipated back into the pool.

Amar uncurled his fist and reached deep into the water as if he could pull Rajahansa back to him. "Raj, Rajahansa, wait, please."

The thinnest essence of Rajahansa's presence rose back to the surface. *Let me go, Amar. My pain is my own, my regret unquenchable.*

"I want to be able to forgive you," Amar said. "But every time I think of Parmver and Aadi, I just can't. What you did to them is beyond my capacity to resolve. But as for what you did to me, I forgive you, Rajahansa. And to make up for the harm you've caused, I intend to take your dragonstone to Stonefountain and use it to save as many people from Khalid as I can. Perhaps somehow in saving their lives, you and I can both find respite from the wrongs you have done."

Take my stone then, Amar. Do whatever good with it you can, and . . . tell Indumauli I'm sorry. He believed in me when no one else did anymore. He trusted me long past when he should have turned away.

"I'll tell him, Raj."

A ghostly claw reached up through the water to envelop Amar's hand. *Farewell.* Rajahansa vanished back into the deepest heart of the mountain. Amar lifted his hand from the pool and watched the water droplets trickled down his hand and arm.

"Farewell, my friend."

Chapter Ten

Lord Jesson's dragon settled onto the roof of the All Council meeting hall in the center of Daro. Khalid glared around him at the city of mud brick buildings, so primitive, so squalid, it was an affront to civilized men that people would live this way.

This world has fallen into savage degradation, Khalid told the dragon. *Amar, the Nagas who follow him, and the humans can't possibly wish to continue to live like bovinders wallowing in their own filth. Why do they resist me? I'm trying to restore all that was good in this world.*

Jesson's dragon made no reply. The beast had made no attempt to resist Khalid's control of it, but it had stolidly refused to communicate with Khalid as if he were his true Naga.

Sulk all you want, Khalid told the dragon. *We are about to do what all my guardsmen failed at. Those dragon hunters are here, and I intend to drive them out into the open.* Khalid spread his mind out across the city, sensing the thoughts and intents of the humans. Their minds were so petty, so simple, they could not hide any of their deepest desires or darkest secrets from him. He perceived everything, and to his great annoyance found Lord Jesson had not exaggerated. There was not even a glimmer of rebellion in their minds. He felt nothing more than the usual human discontent and mulishness.

You human drivel, he roared into their minds, sending the force of his thoughts out so every human in the city heard him like the cut of a knife through their own thoughts. *I know some of you are planning to rebel against the king. If you rebels do not surrender and turn yourselves over to justice, I will kill every living soul in this city. The killing starts now and will not end until this city is no more than a tomb unless you stand forth and accept your punishment.*

Khalid seized control of a thousand human men and forced them to arm themselves with whatever sharp implement they had at hand and kill everyone in their houses. Then he marched them out into the streets in search of their neighbors and friends.

Stop! Lord Theodoric's mind burst free from its shielding, grappling with Khalid's to break his control of the humans. The might of Theodoric's power was joined by Kharishi's and another Naga Khalid did not know.

It's LaShawn, Lord Jesson's dragon burst out in surprise. *Lord Theodoric's oldest son. He's supposed to be dead.*

Then I'll kill him right this time. Khalid called forth the full strength of his power against the three lesser minds that had revealed themselves against him. One-by-one he got control of the Nagas' minds and froze them in place. He drew his sword and had Jesson's dragon fly him to them. He found them in the courtyard of the dragon hunter jati complex. The three Nagas—father, son, and grandson—stood shoulder to shoulder in the courtyard, their weapons drawn but unusable, transfixed as the men were by Khalid's power.

Wary, Khalid circled above them, searching the complex for the minds of other rebels who would stand against him. The dragon hunters had to be somewhere close by, but Khalid could not feel them. Theodoric and his family stood alone, easy prey.

Khalid landed and dismounted so he could cut the three men down with his sword. As he approached Theodoric, Khalid heard a scuffling behind him and turned in time to see the blood red of Kumar Raza's armor before a crossbow bolt hit Lord Jesson in the chest. A second bolt followed straight to Lord Jesson's forehead.

Khalid howled in rage as his spirit tore free of Lord Jesson's body. Lord Jesson and his dragon followed him in death as his spirit and theirs fled back to Stonefountain.

Devaj, Khalid bellowed into the broken mind of the Naga prince, *come now*. A few minutes later Devaj entered the fountain chamber and came trembling to the water. He moaned in despair as Khalid took possession of his body once more.

"Kumar Raza!" he shouted. "Raza, where did you come from?" There had been no sign of the man's mind, not even the slightest glimmer of his existence. Khalid's rage settled into an ominous fire. There could be only one explanation. Somehow the humans had found a way to shield their presence from him. The missing humans were not dead. They were very much alive, just hidden. Khalid clenched his fists. How many had Jesson reported missing? Five hundred? A thousand? Could there be more? And if Khalid could not feel them, he could not control them. General Chandran and Qadim had succeeded in building an army under the very noses of Khalid's men. And Kuma Raza was leading them.

Khalid's first thought was to send the entire Naga Guard to fight them. The guardsmen had been trained to fight humans who carried singing stones; they could fight Raza's army as well, no matter what they were using to shield their minds.

"But no." Khalid stepped out of the fountain and strode into the palace. Why give Raza such an easy target? He had broken cover to come to the defense of the humans at Daro, just as Khalid had predicted he would. Raza and his men would gladly kill the guardsmen, but they would not be as quick to kill other humans.

"All right, Raza," Khalid said. "You want a war. I'm going to let you fight a war. Humans against humans. Do you think I care if the humans slaughter each other?" Khalid laughed. "No."

Then he grew thoughtful. There were guardsmen at Stonefountain plotting against him as well. It seemed obvious Amar would try to use these men to free the minds of Khalid's human army. The guardsmen would turn against him. How many? How many could he trust to fight honorably by his side? How many were traitors?

Taral! he shouted. *Attend me at once.*

Yes, Your Majesty, Taral answered and sped toward the palace.

Khalid clenched his sword hilt. "It won't work, Amar. The men you count on to help you will be dead before you ever enter this city."

Kumar Raza lowered his crossbow and swore. "He saw me. Theodoric, are you all right?"

"I'm fine." Theodoric sheathed his sword and stretched his arms as if they had been frozen in place for a moment.

"Did he have time to tell anyone anything?" Kumar Raza asked. An angry sweat dampened his clothes beneath his armor. Theodoric had told him what the Naga guardsman had been doing to people in the city.

"That wasn't Jesson," LaShawn said, his face flushed.

"By the fountain, there's no way Jesson could have over-powered all three of us."

Kumar Raza's hand tightened on his crossbow and gazed at the fallen Naga and his dragon. "What?"

"It was Khalid," Theodoric said. "In person or in control of Jesson."

"Then he knows. He knows, and we're not ready. We have lost any advantage of surprise." Kumar Raza gritted his teeth and looked toward Stonefountain.

Karishi cleared his throat. "If Khalid was in Jesson's body, and you killed Jesson, does that mean Khalid is dead? If Khalid was in Jesson's body, where's Devaj? Is he dead?"

"Technically, Khalid is already dead," LaShawn said. "Can he be killed again?"

"We don't have time for this discussion right now." Kumar Raza slung his crossbow onto his back. "We have a dead Naga and dragon too close to our headquarters. In a moment every Naga in Daro is going to be here. We have to move now."

The air above Daro rippled in a dozen places.

"Get inside, go." Kumar Raza motioned for Theodoric and the others to take cover. They sprinted with Kumar into the main building. "To arms," Kumar shouted to the men inside. "We may have to do battle here and now. Sound the horns to gather the army."

"I don't think the guardsmen will come against us," LaShawn said. His face had gone from ruddy to deathly pale. "Why fight us when they have a whole city full of humans to attack us with? You saw how Khalid used the people against us."

Kumar Raza's muscles tensed rock hard. He took a deep breath, waiting for his mind to respond to that thought. He'd not counted on having to deal with human armies until he reached Stonefountain. "By the fountain, we have to get out of the city. We've got to march for Stonefountain right now. Theodoric, tell Amar."

"Maybe we should stay and fight here," LaShawn said. "If we run, we'll have an army of humans from Daro at our back and another army in front of us. We'll be pinned on the savannahs and slaughtered."

Kumar Raza ignored him. Either way they were outnumbered. Their only chance was to move swiftly.

Qadim and General Chandran raced into the room followed by Bolivar and Stonebiter. "What's going on?" Chandran demanded. "You gave the order to sound the horns and gather the army. We're supposed to be bringing everyone together in secret and moving out of the city under cover of darkness."

"Khalid knows we're here," Kumar Raza told them. "I have no doubt he'll mobilize the people of the city against us. I'd rather make our stand at Stonefountain than here. Theodoric believes there are Nagas at Stonefountain who will fight on our side. We're going to need their help to even the odds."

Kumar Raza's military leaders fell silent, their faces blanching.

"Get your men moving now!" Kumar Raza snapped. That startled them into action. Only General Chandran remained behind for a moment.

"Will Amar and Kanvar meet us there?" Chandran asked.

Theodoric stepped forward. "I just told Amar what happened. He says they'll meet us on the savanna. He's worried we'll be slaughtered before we ever reach Stonefountain if he doesn't come straight to our aid."

"Will it make any difference when they do come?" Chandran asked. "Even with their strength, we'll still only have a handful of Nagas against Khalid and all of the Naga guardsmen. I hate to say this, but it might be best for our men to scatter and hide. Why give Khalid's armies a single target if we know we can't defeat him this way? Without the singing stones, we need more time to build a bigger army."

Kumar Raza swallowed hard. He'd agreed to take command because he was a symbol of strength the soldiers could rally around. He had no real experience in leading an army, and what General Chandran said made sense. It would be better to fight on their own terms than to let Khalid push them into a position where they'd be surrounded and slaughtered.

"No, Chandran," Theodoric said. "Kanvar is telling me to keep our army together and march for Stonefountain. He says he has a plan and a weapon that will make up for the loss of the singing stones. He thinks we should fight now, because we may never be this strong again."

"He calls this strong? Does he understand we don't begin to have enough men to fight all of the humans Khalid can bring against us?" Kumar Raza said. Chandran nodded in agreement.

"Take off your helmet for a moment," Theodoric said.

Kumar Raza gave him a guarded look. "The Nagas in the city will feel my mind."

"It doesn't matter now, does it," Theodoric said. "I will not let them take control of you. Do it, Kanvar needs to talk to you."

Kumar Raza raked his fingers through his beard in agitation then pulled the helmet off his head.

Grandfather. Kanvar's voice cut through his mind more clearly and powerfully than ever before. *Take the army to Stonefountain. Trust me. We need to do this now.*

What are you doing? Kumar Raza thought back to him. *What have you done? Why can I hear you so well? I'm not a Naga. Kanvar, explain.*

Kanvar laughed. *Akshara was a very powerful dragon. I'm using his dragonstone to amplify my power. We have other dragonstones as well. I think it's our best chance. We must take this fight to Stonefountain now.*

Kumar Raza acknowledged Kanvar's commands and turned his attention back to General Chandran. "General." Kumar Raza put the helmet back on and grabbed his spears from the rack where they waited. "Kanvar tells me he's discovered a way to defeat Khalid. We need to march against Stonefountain now. I think we should trust him. But it's your call. We can't afford to have conflict between us. If we don't stand united against Khalid, we have no chance of success."

"Kanvar thinks we can win? Is he crazy?" General Chandran's knuckles went white as he gripped his sword hilt.

"I have no doubt that he's crazy." Kumar Raza chuckled. "I also have no doubt that he's right. If you could feel the power he's wielding the way I just did, you would not doubt either."

General Chandran's brow furrowed.

"Has Kanvar ever let you down or failed to do what he promised he'd do?" Kumar Raza asked.

General Chandran's frown deepened for a moment then his face relaxed. "Kanvar." His voice was full of fond emotion. "Kanvar, the weak little crippled boy I took in off the streets of Maran because I feared he would die if left on his own. Kanvar." He laughed, but tears glinted at the edges of his eyes. "Kanvar has proven me wrong about things I thought he couldn't do more times than I can count. All right, Raza. We'll do this. We'll fight. For once I will trust that Kanvar can perform as promised. But it doesn't seem reasonable that a boy so young and crippled, bound to a dragon so old and frail, could defeat the most powerful Naga who has ever lived."

"Well, he most certainly can't do it if he doesn't have the help of his friends and family. Come on, General, let's meet him at Stonefountain."

Chapter Eleven

Kanvar knelt on the banks of the Black River and waited for Indumauli. The jungle was strangely quiet, and a soft rain pattered down through the canopy. Night was starting to fall. The task Kanvar had sent Indumauli to do was perhaps the worst he could ever ask of anyone, and yet so much of Kanvar's plan hinged on this he'd had no choice but to involve the Great Black serpent. If there had been more time, Kanvar could have done it a different way. It had been his plan to hunt enough lesser black serpents he could sew their hides together to make it seem like Taral had killed Indumauli and taken his skin to present to Khalid. But time had run out. Kanvar stroked his crossbow, which rested in the harness on his back. It made him feel better knowing he carried it, though he doubted he'd get to use it. The battle he intended would be fought up close and with a different weapon.

At last, the water rippled and Indumauli crawled up onto the bank beside Kanvar, carrying the iron coffin Karishi had fashioned while experimenting with the effects of iron on Naga powers. Indumauli had retrieved the coffin from Karishi's work room under the mountain by going up through the underground lake. Being polite, Kanvar kept his gaze averted from Indumauli's malformed head where Khalid's sword had struck him. Aadi had not exaggerated how sensitive Indumauli was about the scar.

"You got it?" Kanvar rested his hand against the coffin.

It's in the coffin, Indumauli said. *I'd prefer that Amar did not see it. It's best that he believes you went ahead with your original plan.*

"Thank you, Indumauli." Kanvar said. "Are you . . . all right with this?"

I told you I was before I did it, Indumauli hissed. *My father was loyal to Amar's father all his life and died trying to avenge his murder at the hands of those Naga hunters. He would not mind aiding you now. It is only Amar that I worry about. You know how he is.*

"Yes, I know." Kanvar smiled at the thought of his father. "None of this is easy for him. Are you ready?"

Yes. I'll meet you on the coast. Indumauli slid back into the water. Kanvar stood and looked down at the heavy coffin. He certainly wouldn't be able to carry it. Bensharie dropped down through the trees in the clear space over the river, snatched the coffin up in his back talons, and took it to the cliff ledge where Dharanidhar sat.

Dragonbound IX

Kanvar waited patiently for Bensharie to return and carry him up as well. He could have limped back to the village and climbed the rope to the platform and from there struggled his way up the long staircase in the rock to the ledge, but that would have taken him far too long. As much as Kanvar preferred to do things himself and show no weakness, he just didn't have time to be that stubborn.

By the time Bensharie settled onto the ledge with Kanvar on his back, Amar, Rajan, Tana, Aadi, and Denali were already waiting. Kanvar dismounted, and Amar handed him a shield fashioned from Dharanidhar's cast-off scales. In the center, taking up most of the space of the shield, Amar had set Akshara's dragonstone.

Kanvar accepted the shield from his father and slid it onto his good arm, so the back of the stone itself rested against his skin. Akshara's stone was far too large for Kanvar to carry with his one good hand, too large even to fit well onto the breastplate of his armor. The shield seemed the best option. To keep Kanvar's arm from growing tired from bearing the shield for an extended period of time, Amar had also affixed a clasp to the back that could be locked onto a chain around Dharanidhar's neck, so either Kanvar or Dharanidhar could wield the dragonstone.

"This is nice," Kanvar said. "Heavy, but nice."

"Karishi could have made it lighter," Amar said, "but I don't have his knowledge or skill."

It's magnificent, Dharanidhar rumbled.

In the gray light of the rain-filled sky, Akshara's dragon-stone glimmered a pale blue as Kanvar brushed it gently with his mind. He'd experimented with the power and knew it was not something to be trifled with.

Mahanth's dragonstone pulsed green on Tana's chest, bringing out the green sparkle of her eyes. She had both of her steel jungle knives strapped to her belt, and Kanvar knew she was proficient at using them. Vasanti remained below in the jungle, tasked with defending Mani, Eska, and the rest of the jungle's inhabitants should Kundiland be attacked by Khalid's forces.

Rajan had found the lesser volcanic dragon easily with his mind and taken Bensharie on the short hunt to kill it in its lair while its body was molten hot from basking in the lava. Now Rajan looked truly intimidating dressed in red dragonscale armor, wearing Erebus's dragonstone on his chest. Rajan's dragonclaws were strapped at his belt. His hands rested close to them, but his mind was replaying the goodbye kiss he'd shared with his wife, Dove, and the way Eleanor had clung to him before he'd torn himself away to climb up to the ledge. Embarrassed for intruding on Rajan's personal thoughts, Kanvar turned his mind away.

Denali waited beside Frost. He carried two iron spears as well as his hunting knife, which was sheathed at his waist. The Great White dragonstone hung from a chain around his neck, glimmering like a star, larger than Frost's but equal in brightness.

Dragonbound IX

Hanging back from the crowd, Aadi leaned against the cliff face like a shadow in the fold of the mountain. The shard of Indumauli's dragonstone that he wore was hidden beneath his shirt. He carried no weapons, and Kanvar was concerned about letting him come.

Kanvar slid his hand from the shield, handed it to Dharanidhar, and walked over to Aadi. "Are you all right?"

"I'm as well as ever," Aadi said, frowning.

"You don't have to come. I need Indumauli, but you can stay here."

"I'm coming and you can't stop me," Aadi said.

"You don't have any weapons. I don't want you to get hurt," Kanvar said.

Aadi's hand dropped to his belt, which was hung with a variety of pouches. "I have what I need. I didn't spend all my life studying with Parmver for nothing."

"I'm not sure I understand," Kanvar said.

"Because you have the mushroom brain of a Great Blue dragon. War isn't just about fighting, Kanvar. Someone needs to be there to keep everyone else alive." Stroking the pouches, he gave Kanvar a thin smile.

"You-you know all of Parmver's remedies?"

"I haven't memorized all of them yet," Aadi said, "but I know where he wrote them down. I've looked over his notes and prepared the ones most likely to be needed in battle. In addition, I'm carrying a large supply of Great dragon saliva with me. I'm just one person. I can only do so much, but I intend to do whatever I can for the wounded."

"You're right. You are smarter than I am," Kanvar said. "Thank the fountain you're coming with us."

Kanvar turned away from Aadi and saw that his mother had climbed the stairs and now stood on the last step before the ledge. Her eyes were locked on Amar. Her arms were crossed and she wore a deep frown.

Amar's hand played with the hilt of the sword he wore, which had once belonged to Rajan. Set in Amar's breastplate, Rajahansa's dragonstone glimmered gold. Amar's jaw clenched as he looked over at Mani. Kanvar did not like to see so much tension between his parents.

"Mother." He limped over to the stairs and gazed into her face. He'd avoided his mother since she'd come to the palace to live with Amar. The last they had really spent time with each other, she had told Kanvar to drink the poison that would kill him. When Kanvar had refused, she'd tried to shoot him with Grandfather Raza's crossbow. The shock of his mother's betrayal had never left him. Though he knew he should have long since forgiven her, he'd been unable to do it. Even now as he looked into her pinched face, he found it nearly impossible to speak. "Don't be angry with Father. You know he has to do this. We all have to do this. You tried to kill Father and me once because you believed that Nagas would take over the world and enslave everyone. You did what you thought was right, even though you didn't want to. We don't want to go fight either, but we have to. Khalid is the embodiment of everything you feared about the Nagas. We are not all like Khalid, and because of that we have to fight him no matter what the consequences."

Kanvar took a step closer to his mother and wrapped pleading hand around her arm. "Please," he whispered. "Don't let father go away with you angry at him. This may be the last time you ever see him alive. You love him. I know you do. Make sure he knows it before we leave."

"Kanvar." Mani placed a shaking hand on Kanvar's shoulder. "When did you grow up to be a man?"

"Sometime between when you tried to kill me and now," Kanvar said.

"Kanvar, I'm sorry." Mani grabbed him in a tight hug. "I'm sorry I tried to kill you. I'm sorry you've hated me ever since. Please forgive me. I love you."

Surprised, Kanvar wrapped his good arm around his mother to hug her back. His heart tightened. "I forgive you," he said. "I love you too."

Amar joined them, hugging them both and kissing Mani on the forehead. "I love you, Mani. I'll come back to you. I promise."

The flap of great wings pulled Kanvar away, and he limped to the edge to greet the strongest fighters of the Great Blue dragon pride as they arrived. When Kanvar had told them how he planned to use Akshara's dragonstone to defeat Khalid and free the five Great Blue dragons that were enslaved at Stonefountain, the fighters of the Great Blue dragon pride had been determined to come with him. Kanvar was grateful for their willingness. It solved the most pressing problem of how to get Tana and the other Nagas to Stonefountain. Bensharie could only carry Amar over that distance, and Dharanidhar would be better off only carrying Kanvar and the medicine he would need to be able to fly and fight.

Are you ready? A dragon by the name of Naitik had taken leadership of the pride since Anilon and the others had been captured and taken as slaves to Stonefountain.

"Yes, we're ready," Kanvar said as Dharanidhar lifted him up onto his neck. "Let's fly."

Frost flapped up to sit on Dharanidhar's shoulder.

Amar climbed on Bensharie's back, and the two took to the air. The Great Blue dragons collected the rest of the Nagas from the ledge and fell into formation behind Dharanidhar as he lifted off and started for Stonefountain.

A vicious moon lit the savanna with a pale light, reflecting off the helmets and armor of the soldiers that made their swift march through the night from Daro toward Stonefountain. They traveled in three columns: the men from Darvat led by Bolivar and Stonebiter, the army from Maran led by General Chandran, and the dragon hunters from

Daro led by Qadim. In the air above them, Kumar Raza rode with Theodoric on Ishayu. Karishi rode with his father on Damodar. Tazeran slithered through the grass beneath them, preferring to keep all four of his claws on the ground whenever possible.

Theodoric, LaShawn, and Karishi kept well away from Qadim and his men. The dragon hunters had not been happy to find out there would be Nagas with them, but they could not deny the need for Naga help. If Theodoric and his boys had not fought with all their mental strength against the Nagas in Daro, the army would never have won its way out of the city. The humans in thrall to the guardsmen at Daro were unskilled at fighting and had only weapons such as pitchforks and kitchen knives, but the sheer mass of their numbers would have hemmed Kumar Raza's army in and slaughtered it. The gold dragons' joy breath and the Nagas' bold fight to wrench the human minds away from the guardsmen had worked long enough for the army to fight clear and get on its way.

Kumar Raza was all too aware of how much the fight had weakened Theodoric and his dragon.

"Can Ishayu keep flying?" Kumar Raza asked Theodoric.

"He has no other choice, does he?" Theodoric said.

"I could march with the soldiers if that would be easier," Kumar Raza offered. "Ishayu doesn't have to carry two of us."

"How far is it to Stonefountain? How long will it take us?" Theodoric asked. "I flew a different path when I escaped there with Kanvar."

"It's an easy flight for the dragons," Kumar Raza said. "We could get there by morning. The army will take longer. Two days at the shortest if we march full speed and rest little."

"We'll stay in the air above them for now to turn back any human forces that try to attack us from behind," Theodoric said. "I'd prefer you stayed with me. I don't trust Qadim and his dragon hunters not to attack us."

While Theodoric's dragon crossed back and forth in the air above the soldiers, Kumar Raza scanned the horizon behind them and in front for enemies. It would be nice to get across the savannas without fighting again, but what were the chances Khalid would let them do it?

In the early hours of the morning, General Chandran brought the army to a stop to rest. They had not had time to gather provisions to last for more than a couple of days. A long slow trek across the savannas would only hurt them. But they had to rest for a while and eat to regain their strength enough to continue. Just as Ishayu was spiraling toward the ground, Kumar Raza saw a black spot on the horizon, a single dragon and Naga winging toward them. The dragon's flight was unsteady as if it were injured.

"Theodoric." Kumar Raza pointed at the Naga headed their way. "See who it is. He looks hurt."

Theodoric tensed, and Ishayu rose back into the air where Kumar Raza could get a clear shot at the coming Naga with his crossbow. Theodoric spoke a few moments later.

"It's a guardsman named Fistas. I don't know him well. He's hurt and says His Majesty Amar sent him to us, since we're the closest that can give him aid."

"Check with Amar, make sure he's telling the truth," Kumar Raza said. "Hold your fire," he called down to the soldiers as the Naga drew closer.

"His Majesty says Fistas is one of the guardsmen that planned to stand with us at Stonefountain." Theodoric urged Ishayu to fly out and meet the faltering dragon and rider.

"Land," Kumar Raza called out to Fistas.

Fistas's dragon settled to the ground with a groan. A gash in his side oozed blood. Why didn't he lick it closed? Kumar Raza wondered as he dismounted and rushed over to the Naga that the dragon lifted from his neck and laid on the ground. A crossbow bolt stuck out from Fistas's side. The shaft was slicked with blood as if Fistas had been try-ing to pull it free. "I can't get it out," Fistas said, panting in pain and weakness. "It's lodged in my ribs." No wonder the dragon hadn't licked the wound closed.

"What happened?" Theodoric asked as Kumar Raza dropped down beside Fistas to get a better look at the wound.

"Khalid is . . . slaughtering the guardsmen one-by-one in secret. Tearing their minds apart to find the ones he thinks will betray him. I-I wiped everyone's minds that I knew of. He won't find anything about His Majesty Amar or our plans from them. But I couldn't wipe my own mind. I had to run. Khalid has given standing orders that if anyone even looks like they're coming to help you, they are to be killed instantly. My brother shot me. He's on our side; he just can't remember that right now."

Kumar Raza drew his hunting knife. "I'm going to have to cut the wound open a bit and pry the head of the bolt out of the bone. This is going to hurt."

"No," Theodoric said, reaching a hand out to Fistas's forehead. "This won't hurt. Just give me a moment. Fistas, relax and let me enter your mind."

Fistas gritted his teeth and nodded.

Kumar Raza waited for Theodoric to give him word before cutting the crossbow bolt free and healing the wound over with Great dragon saliva. Fistas lay quiet and still while Kumar Raza worked. When Kumar Raza finished, he wiped the blood from Fistas's torso. Theodoric took off his own shirt and gave it to Fistas to replace his torn and bloody one.

"No, My Lord," Fistas tried to resist Theodoric's gift, but Theodoric would not be dissuaded.

Kumar Raza helped Fistas get the shirt on and let him back gently to the ground. "You erased the memories of the guardsmen who would have helped us, who would have fought against Khalid, all of them?" Kumar Raza asked.

Fistas nodded. "I'm sorry. I had to. He would have murdered them all."

"So they will only fight for Khalid now?" Kumar Raza's gut twisted. Khalid had done it again. Despite all their careful plans, he'd outmaneuvered them once more.

Fistas gritted his teeth. If his face could have gotten any paler it would have. "I did not have time to set a trigger in their minds. Yes, we've lost them all except . . . my brother, Taral. His memories will return on contact with Amar's mind. But it would be cruel to let him remember now. He made me promise I wouldn't let him hurt anyone if I wiped his mind. I failed to keep that promise. There was no way I could. Khalid has been using Taral to bring the guardsmen to the palace in secret. Taral has helped with the interrogations and acted as Khalid's executioner. My brother is the gentlest, the most noble . . . but Khalid has twisted him to the most heinous evil. He will never be able to live with himself if he remembers who he truly is."

"If this inquisition is being held in secret, how did you find out?" Kumar Raza asked. He did not doubt Fistas's sincerity, but he feared Khalid was using the man against them somehow.

"I've been keeping track of my brother. I promised him I would. Only . . . I failed him."

"Leave him alone, Raza," Theodoric said. "I've been inside his mind. Khalid has no hold on it. Rest now, Fistas. Don't worry. You're going to be all right."

"None of us are going to be all right. Khalid has already won," Fistas said.

Kumar Raza left Fistas in Theodoric's care and stalked away. He considered warning Chandran, Bolivar, and Qadim that the help they'd planned to get at Stonefountain would not be there, but what good would telling them do? They'd come too far. Their army was out in the open now. It couldn't melt away into the city and vanish. They had to move forward and finish what they'd started.

"Kanvar," Kumar Raza mused, fingering his crossbow. "I hope whatever you've planned is enough to make up for losing the help of the guardsmen."

Chapter Twelve

Kanvar groaned as Dharanidhar lifted him from his neck and set him on the ground on the cost of Varna. Morning sunlight glimmered on the horizon. A stiff breeze blew gritty sand into Kanvar's face. "I feel like an old man," Kanvar said, stretching his aching body.

You are an old man, Dharanidhar rumbled. *Just think, you could have bonded with Bensharie and remained young for hundreds of years.*

"Then who would my father be bound to now?" Kanvar watched as Bensharie settled to the ground followed by the Great Blue dragons. Amar slid from Bensharie's back and headed for Kanvar.

True. Bensharie and your father are good for each other. Kanvar . . . Dharanidhar lowered his head to the ground so Kivi's eyes would be close to Kanvar's face. Kanvar smiled up at the lesser green serpent, knowing only through Kivi's eyes could Dharanidhar see him.

"What, Dhar?"

I am old. It's not right that your life should be so short. When I die, I want you to try and bond with a younger dragon. Assuming my life doesn't end tomorrow, you should have plenty of time to find someone you'd be compatible with.

"I'm more likely to be killed tomorrow than you. Too bad there is not another Naga you could use to replace me. But, Dhar, seriously, even if we both live until you die of old age, I have no desire to continue in this life without you. When we die, whether that's tomorrow or a hundred years from now, we will go together. Agreed?"

Dharanidhar bared his teeth and growled.

"There's no use arguing about it," Kanvar said. "I've already made up my mind, and you won't change it."

"Arguing about what?" Amar asked as he reached Kanvar. "There's no need to argue. I know Dharanidhar will have to rest here for some time before flying again."

Kanvar let out a tight laugh. He had no intention of telling his father what he and Dharanidhar had been discussing. "Of course, we have to rest, but you do not. Take the blue dragons and fly toward Daro. Find General Chandran and my grandfather and stay with them. Make sure they reach Stonefountain safely and get ready to attack. You understand what you have to do, right? Show yourself to the guardsmen and rally those who would join you. Get them to free the minds of the human armies so our army won't be outnumbered."

Amar shook his head. His face was pale, and he had a bleak look in his eyes that had not been there when they'd left Kundiland. "There are no guardsmen left who will fight with us. Khalid has either killed or taken control of them all. Only Fistas survived, though he was severely wounded. I sent him to Kumar Raza."

A cold chill swept over Kanvar. "What about Taral?"

"Khalid has full control of his mind. He's twisted it every bit as much as he did Rajahansa's. Fistas said he planted a trigger. When Taral hears my command he might remember he's sworn himself to my service and obey it. Or he might be too far gone to respond at all." Amar rubbed Rajahansa's dragonstone set in his breastplate. "I don't know what to do, Kanvar. The army is exposed. Theodoric says we have no choice but to fight now. Do you think we will be strong enough with the dragonstones to free the human army and grapple with the minds of the guardsmen at the same time?"

Kanvar looked over at the Great Blue dragons. "That would be foolish to attempt. It could never work even with the dragonstones. Instead you must concentrate on keeping the Great Blue dragons' minds free: the ones that are with you, and the ones already captive at Stonefountain. Free them, keep them free, and have them fight the Naga Guard. The guardsmen have swords and crossbows, but those are little use against mature Great Blue dragons in flight. The guardsmen's gold dragons have joy breath, but these blues have a great deal of experience fighting gold dragons. They know how to hold their breath to avoid being dazed."

Amar's brow furrowed as he tried to take in what Kanvar was telling him. "What about the human armies? They will overrun our soldiers by sheer force of numbers."

"We have three gold dragons on our side: Ishayu, Bensharie, and Damodar. They can immobilize the enslaved human soldiers with their joy breath. Not all of them at once, of course, but if you concentrate the joy breath on the humans on the front lines, it should protect our army for a time, and time is all we need."

"Assuming Lord Taral responds to my command."

"If he does not, I will find a way to get to Devaj and stop Khalid anyway. I promise you, Father. You need only keep the Naga Guard and their army engaged long enough for me to banish Khalid back to the fountain." Kanvar patted the iron box in a pouch at his waist. "Then I will cut his stone free from the fountain and imprison it, so he can never possess anyone else. It will work. I promise. It has to."

Amar looked away across the horizon toward Stonefountain. "I hope tearing him from the fountain does not leave the other spirits in too much torment."

"Khalid's spirit poisons the fountain. I imagine the others will be relieved to have him taken, even if it hurts a bit."

Amar shuddered. "And Devaj?"

"I will not kill Devaj, I promise you. How could I? It takes all my strength to lift the shield. I could not possibly wield any other weapon against him at the same time."

"And what's to stop Khalid from fighting you? The king's sword can cut through that shield."

"Father." Kanvar clasped Amar's hand. "I will fight Khalid, and I will win. Now take the others and go help Grandfather and his army. Indumauli, Dhar, and I will wait here until nightfall and then move into position. As soon as you give me word that the army is ready to attack Stonefountain, I'll go after Khalid."

Amar grimaced and clenched his fist. "I suppose we have no other choice."

No, there is no other choice, Dharanidhar rumbled. *We will have freedom or death.*

Wordlessly, Amar returned to Bensharie and gave the command for the Great Blue dragons to follow him. Tana waved to Kanvar from the foreclaw of the dragon who carried her. *Be well, Kanvar. May the power of Stonefountain sustain you.*

Kanvar smiled through gritted teeth and waved back.

From atop Saanjh's back, Taral watched the human army march toward Stonefountain. The men had an eerie ghostly quality to them. Taral could see close to a thousand men marching in three columns, but he could feel nothing.

Like an army of dead men, Saanjh rumbled. *The dead come to fight the dead king of Stonefountain.*

Taral grinned. He'd sent enough traitor guardsmen's spirits to the fountain to make up for Khalid's having left it. The smell of their blood still clung to him, though he'd washed after a night full of cold satisfaction. Taral let his gaze linger on the ghostly army. At this pace, they would arrive outside of Stonefountain by nightfall. Come morning, the ragged band of humans would face the might of Stone-fountain and be utterly slaughtered.

Saanjh licked his lips. *Khalid did promise us a few prisoners to deal with at our leisure.*

Taral grinned.

Saanjh adjusted his flight to swing back to Stone-fountain. A flash of blue caught Taral's eye, and he turned his head to watch a full flight of Great Blue dragons speed across the sky toward the human army. Roaring, the dragons circled above the men but did not attack.

Your Majesty. Taral sent his thoughts out to the king, hoping his intrusion would not anger Khalid.

What? Khalid was enjoying a lavish meal of roasted tri-horn and stuffed itchekin. He seemed to be in a pleasant mood, which was a relief after the intensity of the night before.

The Great Blue dragon pride has just joined the rebels.

Dragonbound IX

Can you feel their minds, or are they hidden like the humans'? Khalid took a drink of wine and dabbed his lips with a napkin.

I can feel them. Should I take control and have them attack the humans? That would be entertaining.

Khalid laughed. *Go ahead, Taral. Let me see what happens through your eyes.*

Focusing his thoughts, Taral reached out to the Great Blue dragons, intending to wrench their minds to his control. He hit a burning shield. The moment his mind touched it, the shield exploded into his thoughts like a volcano spewing molten lava over his body. He screamed and tried to block the flow of fire, but his strength was no match for the power that grabbed him and dragged him down to the heart of the volcano. A Naga voice like the roar of a red dragon blasted through him. *The Great Blue dragons are mine, and you will not touch them!*

At the back of his mind, Taral heard Khalid swear. Khalid wrenched Taral free of the burning fire and threw up a shield to protect him. *Return to Stonefountain*, Khalid ordered. *Do not engage the human army alone again. That was Rajan. He's grown more powerful somehow. You must combine your strength with that of the other guardsmen to defeat him. But not now. We will wait until he has to contend with our human army as well. The chaos of battle and the slaughter of his human friends will distract him. Then we will strike him down.*

As Saanjh whirled in the air and winged for Stonefountain, Khalid's mind withdrew, leaving Taral alone. He stiffened, fearing a further attack by Rajan, but Rajan had retreated back behind his own shields. Taral glanced down at his arms and chest, expecting his clothes to be burned off and his body blackened by the lava. He looked no different than he had before he'd engaged with Rajan. Still, the feel of the punishing burns persisted. He sucked in a slow breath. *Perhaps the battle tomorrow will not go as easily as we thought*, he told Saanjh.

Saanjh growled in agreement. As they flew back to the city, they passed their own army mustering in the fields outside of town. Their forces outnumbered the rebels by more than ten to one. But Rajan and the Great Blue dragons would be a problem.

Come, Taral called the captains of the Guard. With Lord Jesson dead, Khalid had raised Taral to head of the Elite Guard, which gave him command of all the Naga guardsmen. *Things have changed. We have a battle to plan.*

Hours later, Saanjh settled into the courtyard of Taral's mansion. The human army was gathered, the sentries set. All was in readiness for the morning. Taral strode into his chambers and noticed a small kitrat curled up on the pillow of his bed.

"Giri!" he shouted. "What is this kitrat hatchling doing here? I told you to get rid of it."

Giri hurried into the room and snatched up the hatchling. It mewled and climbed up the sleeve of Giri's shirt. "Forgive me, My Lord. I've thrown it out. It just keeps coming back. Perhaps if you let me feed it and keep it in my own room, it would not bother you."

"Have you seen Aadi today?" Taral once again searched Giri's mind for any sign of the halfblood boy. Taral desperately wanted to get his hands on Aadi so he could enjoy his suffering at least a little before turning him over to Khalid. He caressed the halfblood dagger he carried tucked in his belt. A cold mist crept up his arm, and he wondered what would happen if he cut Aadi with it just a little. Not enough to kill, just enough to make Aadi wish it would.

"No, My Lord. Still no sign of him. I have a meal prepared for you in the dining room."

Hours later, in the depth of the night, a faint sound snapped Taral's eyes open. He heard the slosh of water, the click of serpent claws on flagstones, and the rasp of a scaly body. Leaping from his bed, he drew his sword, and glanced through his window out to the courtyard. A puddle of black glimmered in the moonlight, great black coils that uncurled from around a man in blue armor and some kind of metal coffin. Both man and serpent were shielded from Taral's mind.

Taral exchanged his sword for his crossbow, loaded it, and sighted his target through the window. He'd kill the serpent first. Indumauli's poison was more dangerous than an attack from any man, especially one as strange as this. Perhaps it was the shadows writhing in the moonlight, but it appeared like the man's left arm was only a useless stump and his left leg was twisted.

Taral lifted his crossbow to shoot the serpent between the eyes.

Hold your fire, a warm voice slid into Taral's mind. The shock of it jerked his hand and the crossbow went off, but the surprised movement had ruined his aim and the bolt sailed over the serpent's head. The man swore and ducked down behind the coffin.

Taral tried to reload, but the serpent shot across the courtyard and in through his window, slapping the crossbow out of his hands and wrapping tight coils around him. Yelling for Saanjh to wake up and come to his aid, Taral struggled to reach his sword. The serpent bared its fangs and hissed in his face.

Taral froze. One nick of those fangs could end his life without instant access to Great Dragon saliva. *Close your mouth*, Taral ordered the serpent, trying to use his powers to control the monster, but Indumauli's mind remained shielded from his control. Desperately, he tried to break through the shield while the serpent's head swayed back and forth in front of his face, the fangs coming ever closer to him.

Taral. The warm voice entered his mind again. It seemed familiar somehow, but he couldn't place it. *Taral, this is King Amar. I command you to stop fighting and listen to me.*

Taral's mind spun, his thoughts clashed in chaos as new memories rushed in upon him. It was as if the mind of some other man had invaded his own and was fighting to shatter his very sense of existence. He screamed in mental anguish. *What are you doing to me? Who are you? Stay away. Kha—*

His attempt to call Khalid for help cut off as the man in blue armor limped into the room with a glowing blue shield on his arm. The man's Naga power, augmented by the shield somehow, wrapped around him and bound his mind so tightly no one would hear him no matter how hard he screamed. He turned to Saanjh for help, but found Saanjh bound just as tightly.

The golden presence that had spoken previously melted into his mind with greater force. *Taral, this is King Amar. You have sworn yourself to my service. You must remember now who you are and what you've agreed to do.* A clear memory of standing on a rainy beach before a man with golden armor and a golden crown, glowed to life in Taral's mind. He heard himself say, "My King. I will seek the gold dragonstones, return to Stonefountain, and do everything you ask."

Around him ten young gold dragons huddled in starvation. He drew his sword, but he did not kill them. Instead, he fed them and handed them over to the golden king to take to safety.

I don't understand, Taral whimpered. *I killed them, every last one, and carried their dragonstones to Khalid.*

King Amar pushed his mind in another direction, revealing another hidden memory. Instead of killing the young dragons, he and Saanjh had dug up the stones from some ancient burial ground.

No, you're lying. Taral forced Amar's mind back out of the depths of his own. *If you are King Amar, then you are my enemy. I care nothing for your worthless imaginings. I will not listen to dreams you want to plant in me to take control. I do not serve you. I never have, and I never will.*

Amar's mind relented. *We've lost him, Kanvar,* he spoke to the man in blue armor. *I don't know what we can do.*

Kanvar? Taral thought. *So you are the abomination, traitor, who would try to unseat the king. You crave the throne for yourself and would kill your own brother to take it.*

Kanvar laughed. *Don't worry, Father. Lord Taral will be just fine. Leave him to me now. Break off, before Khalid feels you. Go.*

Are you sure? Amar's worried thoughts eased away from Taral's mind.

I promise, he'll be all right, Kanvar said. *Taral's memories have returned. It will only take me a moment more to convince him to accept the truth. Be well, Father. I will see you in person soon.*

King Amar's mind slipped fully away, leaving Taral alone with Kanvar. The Great Blue dragonstone in Kanvar's shield glowed brightly as he pressed it against the side of Taral's head.

"I don't care which king you think you serve," Kanvar said, letting his power soak through every part of Taral's mind. "From now on, you will do exactly what I tell you to."

Taral gasped as free will tore away from him and Kanvar's consciousness overpowered his own.

Chapter Thirteen

From the palace window, Khalid watched as the ragged human army faced off with his larger force. Morning sunlight glittered across the city's streets and mansions and fell on the soldiers. The Naga Guard gathered in the air above the city, staying back from the human armies. Though the Nagas could fight with sword and crossbow, there would be no need for that. Their best weapon against the rebel army was other humans. Khalid grinned. The humans would die today by the thousands. This battle would break them so they would never dare think of rising against him again.

The Great Blue dragons took to the air above the rebels. The smile left Khalid's face. Rajan had come with the blue dragons. Something had increased his power since Khalid had confronted him in Kundiland. Still, the Naga guardsmen vastly outnumbered Rajan. Try as he might to shield the Great Blue dragons, he would be immobilized and destroyed. Then the dragons would be a terror of blood and fire against their own allies. If that failed, the ballistae would finish the blue dragons anyway.

Elkatran. Khalid summoned Devaj's dragon. The pitiful creature was an empty shell, useful only for carrying Khalid through the air. Elkatran came into the chamber and lowered his head, ready for Khalid to mount him.

From his mansion beside the river, Taral rose into the air. His dragon winged toward Khalid with something clutched in his foreclaws. Khalid tensed and drew his sword. As he approached, Taral held his sheathed sword and empty crossbow in the air where Khalid could see them. He tossed both weapons to the floor of the chamber at Khalid's feet before letting his dragon fly through the window and land.

"The men are ready," Taral said as he dismounted and untied a large black bundle from behind his saddle. Both he and his dragon stayed far back from Khalid, knowing the distance Khalid insisted he keep.

"What have you brought?" Khalid asked, keeping his sword ready in his hand. Taral's mind was shielded from him, and he did not like that.

"You gave me a job to do, Your Majesty. At last I have completed it, though I was up most of the night to do it. When the soldiers left the riverside last night, that wretched black serpent sulked out of hiding as I figured he might. This is for you." Taral unfastened the bundle and rolled a

Great Black serpent hide out across the floor. The serpent's black dragonstone lay dark and empty between the serpent's dead eyes. "And this." Taral motioned to Saanjh who set a metal coffin on the ground beside the dead serpent. "I found Aadi's remains in the serpent's lair beneath the river bank. He was so bloated and disfigured it was a messy business getting him out of there. There's not much left to look at, I'm afraid, but I brought him all the same."

Taral bowed. He and his dragon backed away to the far side of the chamber as Khalid strode forward and examined the pelt. "It seems a bit brittle for a fresh kill," Khalid said after a moment. "Are you sure you didn't dig up some other long-dead serpent?"

Taral opened his mind to Khalid and let him see how he'd trapped and killed Indumauli in the river.

"That's a pretty picture Taral, but there's one little problem with it." Khalid tightened his grip on his sword and advanced on Taral. "When Indumauli bit me, I cut away part of his dragonstone and head. This serpent's head and stone are intact."

Taral flinched back against his dragon. "I didn't ask the serpent's name when I killed it. I just assumed it was the one you wanted."

"And the boy in the coffin isn't Aadi, is he, Taral? Did you think you could kill some human boy and then mutilate the remains so I wouldn't be able to tell the difference? But where in this city could you find a boy with the gray skin of a Kundiland native?"

Taral dropped to his knees. "Your Majesty, I swear I found the boy's body in the serpent's lair. It has to be Aadi. Like you said, no one else's skin would be that color. It's true, it's bleached and bloated but still I believe I really did find him." The image of Aadi's remains played in gruesome detail across Taral's mind.

"If that is true," Khalid said, setting the blade of the sword against Taral's throat. "Then you won't mind opening the coffin to show me."

"Of course, Your Majesty. I will do so gladly." With the blade still to his throat, Taral rose, edged to the coffin, undid the clasp, and threw the lid back.

Blue light flashed in Khalid's face, blinding him as Kanvar rose out of the coffin, wielding a Great Blue dragonstone in a shield on his arm, the likes of which Khalid had never seen. It was giant, and the power that surged through it flung itself against Khalid.

"Traitor!" Khalid tried to slice the sword across Taral's throat, but Kanvar slammed the shield against Khalid's arm, numbing it so he dropped the sword.

Now, Father, Kanvar cried out with his mind. *Attack!*

Through the window Khalid saw the human army surge forward. The Great Blue dragons flew directly at the Naga guardsmen. Three gold dragons swept into the air, spewing their joy breath over the front ranks of Khalid's soldiers.

At the same time, Kanvar, wielding the full power of the dragonstone, pressed his attack on Khalid, tearing at

Khalid's consciousness, trying to separate it from Devaj. Khalid fought back with all his strength, but in Devaj's weakened body, linked to the near-powerless Elkatran, Khalid's mind slipped in his grapple with Kanvar's.

Guardsmen! Khalid screamed. *To me, to the king. Forget the blue dragons. Your duty is to defend me.*

Kanvar threw up a shield that prevented his cry from leaving the chamber.

"Taral," Khalid yelled. "Fight him. Kill him."

Taral stood frozen in place, wide-eyed, torn between the two powers that vied for control of his mind.

You will not defeat me. Khalid clawed at Kanvar's mind, but Kanvar blocked it with the power of the shield. Bit-by-bit Kanvar got hold of Khalid's soul and tore it free from Devaj's body.

Return to the fountain, Kanvar ordered. *Return to your grave, Khalid.*

Khalid howled in rage and flung himself at Taral, abandoning Devaj's worthless body in exchange for Taral's practiced sword arm and Saanjh's more powerful bond.

Kanvar heaved a sigh of relief as he felt Khalid's spirit flee Devaj's body. Devaj crumpled to the ground at Kanvar's feet. Kanvar tried to catch his brother before he hit his head on the ground, but the shield weighed his arm down too much. Kanvar dropped to his knees. "Devaj, thank the fountain. He's gone now." Kanvar knew he needed to move to the fountain quickly to cut Khalid's stone free and imprison it, but he wanted to be sure Devaj was all right first.

Devaj's eyes fluttered open and came to rest on something behind Kanvar.

"Kanvar," Devaj let out a weak shout and kicked Kanvar in the side, sending him sprawling to the left just as Taral's sword passed through the air where Kanvar had been.

Kanvar struggled to his feet and raised his shield, blocking a second sword thrust, and using the power of Akshara's stone in an attempt to regain control of Taral's mind. How had he lost it?

Taral laughed and a gold dragonstone appeared in his left hand. "Two can play at that game, boy." A gold-red fire blazed to life in Taral's eyes as he gazed down at the stone in his hand. "Greetings, Sukhderean, old friend. It's time you and I worked together once more."

Kanvar gasped, and the full force of Khalid's mind slammed into him, stronger now that Kanvar had lost the advantage of surprise, and stronger still with Khalid holding the dragonstone. Kanvar staggered backward, raising his shield and focusing his power through Akshara's stone to keep his mind free from Khalid's control.

Khalid lunged, striking at Kanvar with the sword, trying to work his blade past Kanvar's shield at the same time that he clawed at Kanvar's mind with his own. Kanvar used the shield to block sword and mental attack, but Khalid drove him backward toward the window. At least Khalid could not wield the king's sword while in Taral's body. He'd been forced to retrieve Taral's sword from the ground where he'd tossed it before landing.

Kanvar's arm burned with the strain of holding the heavy shield up while blow after blow rained down on him. Gritting his teeth, he pushed back with his mind, once more trying to tear Khalid free from the body he'd possessed.

Behind Khalid, Devaj crawled over to the fallen sword of the king, got his hand on the hilt, and started to rise. With a roar, Saanjh pounced on him, flattening him to the ground, and sending the sword skittering out of his grasp.

Overbalanced by the shield and the strength of Khalid's blows against it, Kanvar tripped and fell backward. The window ledge caught him, but he was pinned against it as Khalid pressed his attack.

Dharanidhar, Kanvar called to his dragon. The drop from the palace window was a long way to the base of the mountain.

I'm trying to reach you. Dharanidhar's answer was cut short by a ballista bolt that grazed his left wing as he spun to dodge. In addition to the ballistae, a half-dozen guardsmen were scattered between Dharanidhar and the palace.

Kanvar rolled to the left, trying to get away from the window, but Khalid stopped him with a sword thrust that pierced his armor and cut into his side. Crying out, Kanvar slammed the shield against Khalid's sword arm while the sword was engaged with his flesh.

Khalid grunted in pain and lost his grip on the sword. It fell to the ground. Sweat streamed down Kanvar's face, stinging his eyes as he shifted to stand over the sword so Khalid could not snatch it back up. Khalid responded with a sharp attack on Kanvar's mind, clawing and rending at his consciousness, crushing Kanvar's will, and digging in deep to freeze his body.

Kanvar fought back with all his might. Akshara's stone was bigger than Sukhderean's. It should be more powerful. But Khalid was older than Kanvar and much more experienced in using the power of his mind as a weapon. Kanvar's focus weakened. Khalid eased Sukhderean's stone toward Kanvar's head. Golden power rushed from it, resonating between Taral, Saanjh, and Khalid and more— somehow Khalid was harnessing the power of Stonefountain itself, forcing the full strength of the Nagas resting there to blast through Kanvar's mind. Kanvar's will wavered as he realized Khalid had been as much of a tyrant to the spirits in death as he had been to the world in life.

Don't give up, Dharanidhar's mind entered Kanvar's, bracing him against the onslaught, but Khalid tore the shield from Kanvar's arm so he lost contact with Akshara's dragonstone.

Don't give up, Kanvar, fight him. Rajan's mind, amplified by the molten fire of Erebus's dragonstone joined Dharanidhar's in shoring up Kanvar's defenses.

Dragonbound IX

Why waste your time on a crippled abomination? Rajan taunted Khalid. *Kanvar's nothing to you. Come out and fight me Khalid. Coward. I'm the one you need to stop.*

Khalid ignored Rajan's attempt to divert him and pressed his advantage, spearing deep into Kanvar's mind and vying for control.

Gritting his teeth against the searing pain Khalid inflicted on him, Kanvar fought back, spurred on by Rajan's voice. *My body might be crippled,* Kanvar said, lashing back at Khalid, *but my mind isn't. I might not be strong or fast, but I have what many lack: endurance and determination.*

Khalid howled in rage and struck harder, intent on shattering Kanvar's mind and leaving him begging for death. Without Akshara's singing stone, the last of Kanvar's shields crumbled.

Keep fighting. A flow of green power spread into Kanvar's mind, easing his pain and buoying his will. *I love you, Kanvar. You don't have to face Khalid alone.*

Tana. Kanvar gasped. *If you and Rajan are helping me, who's fighting the guardsmen?*

Theodoric, LaShawn, and Karishi, a cold white voice answered as it flung itself full force at Khalid. A shiver went up Kanvar's back as Denali and Frost came to his aid, followed by a simple command from the dark shadows of Aadi's mind. *Reset your shields, Kanvar. Around your core first. A simple step, protect your core just like Parmver showed you.*

In the face of Khalid's powerful onslaught, Kanvar, with the aid of his friends, found enough space at the center of his mind to reset his core shields. Khalid could hurt him, but he could not take control.

"You are nothing against my power," Khalid snarled, pulling a silver dagger from his belt. "Even all of you together can't defeat me." He stabbed at Kanvar with the dagger.

Kanvar grabbed his wrist, trying to hold the blade back. A sickly gray mist curled around it and up Khalid's arm, brushing Kanvar's hand. Darkness filled Kanvar's heart, and he wished suddenly for death.

Don't listen to it, Aadi cried. *Your Majesty, help us.*

Amar's mind snapped away from the humans he was trying to protect and joined the others in battle against Khalid. *Khalid, tyrant, I'll not let you take my sons from me.* Amar's warmth and light filled Kanvar, holding back the dagger's dark call.

I already have. Khalid pulled another rush of power from the dragonstone and the fountain. With the might of a thousand Naga dead, he threw a shield up around Kanvar's mind, sending the minds of his father and friends spinning away from him.

Stop, Amar yelled as his presence was flung away. *I command you to stop, Khalid!*

Kanvar found himself alone, panting, pressed up against the windowsill by Khalid who glared at him through the glowing eyes of Taral's face. Though Kanvar struggled to stay Taral's hand, the tip of the dagger inched through the scales of his armor.

Kanvar fought back, kicking and struggling as Khalid tried to claw the shields away from the core of Kanvar's being. Then, Khalid's focus faltered and half-turned from Kanvar as if he were distracted by something in his own mind.

With a cry, Taral turned the dagger away from Kanvar and slammed it into his own chest, piercing his heart.

Taral, traitor, how dare you? Khalid howled.

"You knew I would," Taral said through bloodless lips. "Kanvar, tell Fistas not to grieve. I go willingly to stop Khalid." He sagged to the ground, falling away from Kanvar.

Kanvar watched in horror as a gray mist spun up from the blood-soaked dagger, enveloping Taral, filling the room to encompass Saanjh and then sucking back into the dagger, pulling the souls of dragon and men in with it. Shouting, Khalid tried to resist, but Taral wrapped his soul around Khalid's and dragged it into the dagger with him and Saanjh.

Don't touch the dagger, Taral's ghostly voice whispered to Kanvar before disappearing. The room fell silent.

Kanvar pressed his hand against his mouth and staggered away from Taral's lifeless body, but his gaze was drawn back to the silver handle of the dagger that protruded from Taral's chest. He should pull it out. It would dishonor the dead to leave it there. He stepped back toward it, but Taral's warning stayed his hand.

The dagger hissed, and gray smoke swirled around the hilt. Devaj pulled himself out from under Saanjh's dead claws and crawled toward Taral. The dagger whispered indistinctly.

Aadi. Kanvar searched for Aadi's mind through the crowd and press of battle. He found it waiting readily with the others who had been trying to break through Khalid's shields to reach him. *You know this dagger?* Kanvar let Aadi see the image of Taral's body.

By the fountain, don't touch it. Kanvar, don't, Aadi responded in earnest.

Can the spirits come back out of it?

If you touch it, they come . . . inside you. When they're with you, you're no longer alone, but all they want is to force you to join them. Aadi shuddered.

Devaj got to Taral's body and reached for the dagger.

"No." Kanvar lunged at Devaj and wrestled him away.

"Khalid calls me," Devaj sobbed, fighting Kanvar. "I have to obey."

"No you don't. You're free of him. Don't ruin it now." Kanvar got his arm around Devaj's chest and pulled him backwards. The sun dimmed as Dharanidhar's massive form filled the window. He thumped to the chamber floor in an ungraceful landing. Blue fire crackled between his teeth as he lifted Taral's body and placed it gently inside the iron coffin. Then he closed the lid and used the heat of his breath to seal it shut. The iron burned red hot and then died to black before Kanvar released Devaj.

You're bleeding. Dharanidhar pulled Kanvar away from Devaj and peeled his armor back so he could lick the cut on Kanvar's side.

"Stupid dragon," Kanvar said. "Why didn't you just lick your own side and heal both of us." He pulled his armor back down and got to his feet.

Waste of saliva. It takes less to heal you than it does me. Besides, I already licked all the wounds closed that I got in battle. That one was your fault. Dharanidhar lifted Devaj in his foreclaw and brought him up to his face. *Is Khalid still calling you, Your Highness?*

Devaj raked his fingers through his sweat-soaked hair. "I-I can't feel him. I can't hear him. I'm alone. I haven't been alone since . . ."

Since you came to return Kumar Raza's singing stone to the fountain? Dharanidhar rumbled.

Devaj nodded. He was pale and weak, and Kanvar feared he would fall unconscious.

So, trapped in the dagger in the coffin, Khalid has no more control on you? Dharanidhar pressed.

"I can't feel him," Devaj confirmed.

Kanvar, get the shield, Dharanidhar said. *Devaj, will you let Kanvar check your mind just to make sure.*

"No, n-n-no. Kanvar, please don't. My mind is . . . what I've done. You don't want . . . I don't want you to see. I am . . . not your brother anymore. Not the one you knew."

Kanvar looked up at Devaj in Dharanidhar's claw. "I saw the whole of Taral's mind. I'm afraid Father would be angry with me if he knew how forceful I was in enlisting Taral's help. I know Khalid twisted him cruelly, or he twisted himself. Either way, I've seen what Khalid can do to a person. Aadi and Father have as well, and Rajan has his own horrors to grapple with. None of us have been left untainted by evil."

Dharanidhar lowered Devaj to the ground beside Kanvar then picked up the shield and hooked it to the chain around his neck. Kanvar clasped his brother's arm but left his mind alone.

"Kanvar," Devaj's arm shook in Kanvar's grip. "I knew you'd come back for me. Somehow, some way, I knew you'd come."

"If you are not the brother I have known, you are still the brother that I love. But, Devaj, look." Kanvar drew Devaj over to the window where the bloody battle still raged at the edge of the city. Several of the Great Blue dragons had been shot down or forced to turn on their allies by the Naga guardsmen while Amar, Rajan, and the others had turned their attention to the fight with Khalid. The remaining blue dragons were still engaged in aerial combat with the guardsmen. Kumar Raza's army was being overrun by the superior numbers of Khalid's soldiers.

Tears came to Devaj's eyes. "The battle is lost."

"No," Kanvar said. "Dharanidhar and I are going to use Akshara's dragonstone to free the minds of those soldiers. But when we do, the full might of the human armies will turn against the Naga guardsmen. This will turn into the slaughter of Stonefountain all over again unless you stop it."

"Me?"

"You're their king. The guardsmen only take orders from you. You must fly out there and order them to retreat. Tell them to fly for Navgarod. Do not hesitate, do not look back. Devaj, you've got to lead them home."

"My home is in Kundiland," Devaj said, his voice faint. "I do not wish to be king any longer. Tell them they must listen to Father."

"You know they won't," Kanvar said. "Khalid has taken too great of hold on them. If you will not go to Navgarod with them now, tell them to follow Theodoric, and you'll come later. But fly now, Devaj, every moment you wait, more people will die."

Kanvar retrieved the king's sword from where it had fallen and returned it to the sheath at Devaj's side.

"Go. Fly."

Devaj looked over at his dragon. Elkatran had not moved from where he'd lowered his head for Khalid to mount him just before Taral had arrived at the palace. "Kanvar, how can I fly? Elkatran is gone."

Kanvar limped over to the shattered dragon and set his hand on Elkatran's dragonstone. Beneath his touch, Elkatran's mind was blank. "He'll fly if you tell him to, Devaj. And when this is all over, I'm sure we can restore his mind the same way we did Grandfather's. Remember? It can be done."

Devaj climbed on Elkatran's neck and ordered him into the air. As the two winged away from the palace,

Dharanidhar lifted Kanvar up onto his neck. *Freedom or death*, Dharanidhar rumbled, handing Kanvar the shield. Kanvar slid his arm into it and let the full power of Akshara's stone wash through him.

"Freedom or death!" he shouted as Dharanidhar launched himself from the palace window and dove toward Khalid's human armies.

Chapter Fourteen

Freedom or Death! Every human in the city heard Kanvar's rallying cry in their minds. Kanvar knew if the Naga guardsmen united their powers against him, he could be overcome, even with Akshara's stone. But the attacking blue dragons spared him that battle. The compulsion put on the human armies by Khalid and the Naga guardsmen gave way as Kanvar blasted the Nagas' control with Akshara's power, freeing the soldiers' minds.

Naga Guard, to me, to me! Devaj's mind rang out as the humans under their control were freed. The guardsmen tried to break off, but the Great Blue dragons pressed their attack.

Dharanidhar, tell Anilon to let them go, Kanvar said.

Dharanidhar let out a petulant roar. *I'm trying, but they won't follow my commands. They taste Naga blood now and won't pull back.*

The fighting between the two human armies ceased, and the ballistae that had been firing on the Great Blue dragons turned on the golds. As one, the humans focused their attention on the Nagas. Not just the guardsmen, but also the Nagas that had placed themselves in battle against Khalid's armies: Bensharie and Amar; Fistas and his dragon; Theodoric, Ishayu, and Rajan who flew with them; LaShawn and Damodar; Karishi and Tazeran; even Denali and Frost. Tana, and Aadi, having no dragons with them were overlooked, but Kanvar figured that wouldn't last for long. Qadim and his dragon hunters knew Tana was a Naga.

Dharanidhar swore. *Kanvar, what have we done? The humans and blue dragons will slaughter them all.* Dharanidhar roared and dove toward Bensharie and Amar, putting his own body between Bensharie and the ballistae. The sudden attack by their own allies, broke Amar's and the others' concentration. Their shields, which had been keeping the Great Blue dragon's minds from control by the guardsmen, gave way. The blue dragon's minds fell to the control of the Nagas, and the dragons turned back upon the humans, filling the air with scorching blue fire.

Retreat, Devaj called to the Naga guardsmen. *Fly for Navgarod. Retreat, fly, fly. I order you to abandon Stonefountain and return to your homes.*

Father, Bensharie, get out of here, Kanvar said. *You've got to escape to Kundiland or fly with the Naga guard to Navgarod.*

Bensharie broke away from the battle, heading for the west coast. Fistas and his dragon followed. With a sweeping roar, Dharanidhar dove and snatched up Tana and Denali in his foreclaws. Frost took shelter on Dharanidhar's shoulder.

Go with your men, Kanvar ordered Theodoric.

Ishayu lifted Tazeran from the ground with his hind talons and flew toward Kanvar. As Ishayu brushed past Dharanidhar, Rajan leaped from Ishayu's neck onto Dharanidhar's and settled down behind Kanvar, holding on tight so he wouldn't fall. *I don't want to go to Navgarod*, Rajan said. *Dove is waiting for me back in Kundiland.*

Fine, just be careful with those claws, Rajan, you're cutting me. Kanvar winced at the claws Rajan had pressed against his chest with his hand. Rajan eased up his grip, slid the claws off his hands, folded them, and secured them to his belt.

Better?

Yes, where's Aadi? Kanvar scanned the armies below, which had transformed into one angry mob and swept into the city, despite the blue dragon fire that rained down upon them. At last, Kanvar caught sight of Aadi in the company of Raahi and Stonebiter who were moving with the men from Darvat toward the palace. Devaj, Theodoric, LaShawn and Karishi, and the Naga Guard lifted high into the air where the ballistae couldn't reach them and turned westward toward Kundiland. The gold dragon pride from Kundiland abandoned the palace, lifting off with the flutter of gold wings like butterflies startled up from a bush. They surrounded Devaj and winged away to the west.

Freedom or Death, Dharanidhar bellowed and flew toward the Great Blue dragon pride. With the Nagas away safely, Kanvar raised the shield with Akshara's stone and sent out a flash of blue power, freeing the Great Blue dragons' minds.

The Liberator, the Great Blue dragons roared. *The Great Blue Liberator has returned.*

Since the main rush of the human mob was headed toward the palace, Kanvar urged Dharanidhar back there. *Well, we've done it. We've freed them*, Dharanidhar said to Kanvar. *Do you think they'll thank us?*

I don't know, Kanvar answered.

We could just fly away like the others. Dharanidhar circled the palace.

Below them the crowd of humans broke out shouting, "Freedom or Death! The Great Blue Liberator has returned!" Others took up the cry and soon the streets of Stonefountain echoed with the call. "Great Blue Liberator! Great Blue Liberator! Freedom or Death!"

Maybe we should at least try to talk to them, Kanvar said. *Maybe there could be peace between humans and Nagas.*

Dharanidhar let out a doubtful snort but landed in the palace chamber where they'd left Khalid in his iron coffin. Kanvar handed Dharanidhar the shield to put on the chain around his neck.

"Rajan," Kanvar said, stretching his aching arm. "You and the others should stay here. I don't know what's going to happen down there."

Rajan rested his hands on his dragon claws. "If they kill you and Dharanidhar, being up here rather than down there won't make a difference. We won't have a dragon we can fly away on."

"If it looks like things are going badly, get to the river. Indumauli can take you to hide in his lair."

"I'd rather stay with you," Tana said, "whatever happens." Frost and Denali agreed.

Kanvar did not want to put the others in danger, but he could tell they'd never let him face the human armies alone. Dharanidhar let out an irritated roar, lifted the coffin up in his back legs, and flew down to the head of the stairs leading into the palace. He set the coffin on the top step in front of the vanguard of soldiers intent on taking control of the city. Three groups marched up the steps: General Chandran with his top soldiers, Bolivar, Stonebiter, and their men, and Qadim and his dragon hunters. And Kumar Raza, in blood-slicked red armor, led them all. He had his loaded crossbow in one hand, and an iron spear in the other. Raahi and Aadi came up right behind him. Anilon and two others of the Great Blue dragon pride winged down to land by the humans.

Baring his teeth, Dharanidhar settled to the ground behind the coffin. He let Denali and Tana down, then lifted Rajan and Kanvar to the ground. Kanvar limped forward to stand beside the iron coffin. Kumar Raza met him across from it.

"Khalid is no more!" Kanvar shouted so everyone could hear him. "His spirit is sealed in this coffin. As long as no one disturbs it, he will remain trapped in it forever."

Qadim pushed past Raahi and Aadi and strode up the steps to Kumar Raza's side. "You helped the Nagas escape. We could have ended this here and now, but you turned the blue dragons against us so the Nagas can return and finish what they started."

"*I* turned the dragons against you?" Kanvar lifted a hand to the three blue dragons present besides Dharanidhar. "Anilon, is that what happened?"

With a roar, Anilon snatched Qadim in his claw, shook him, and dumped him in a heap on the ground.

"In case you couldn't tell what Anilon was saying," Kanvar said. "What he means is, you idiot, you started shooting at the Nagas who were keeping the blue dragons' minds free from the guardsmen. The blue dragons were turned against you because of your own stupidity. How many soldiers died because you betrayed friends fighting loyally by your side?"

The young dragon hunter named Bitterwood rushed over to help Qadim to his feet. "None of this would have happened if the Nagas hadn't enslaved everyone in the first place," Bitterwood said.

"Wrong again," Kanvar said, pointing to Qadim and General Chandran. "None of this would have happened if you hadn't invaded Kundiland. For a thousand years the Nagas have let you live unhindered in peace. The Naga Guard of Navgarod could have flown over here at any time and conquered your lands. But they didn't. They have no desire to enslave you or rule over you. They only came here because you threatened their king, my father, Amar, who has lived all his life in the seclusion of the Kundiland jungles. You had peace and freedom until you started this war. It was your actions that called Khalid back from the dead and returned his evil to this world."

General Chandran cleared his throat and climbed the steps to stand in front of Kanvar and the coffin. "As much as I want to agree with you, Kanvar, I can't. We rallied our armies because that Naga—" he pointed to Rajan "—infiltrated our government, using his power in an attempt to rule this world."

"He was being controlled by a Great Red volcanic dragon," Kumar Raza said in a low voice with a dangerous edge to it. "The perpetrator of that evil has already paid the price at my hand."

"This finger-pointing is useless," Tana said stepping forward, her green eyes flashing. "What happened in the past does not matter now. The question that lies before us is can we come to a peace agreement or will Nagas and humans continue to fight for another thousand years? Will you raise armies and forge weapons of bloodshed forever, or will you go home to your families and live in peace?"

"We would love to live in peace," General Chandran said. "But how can we, knowing there are Nagas around who could take control of our minds whenever they choose?"

Kanvar smiled, reached across the coffin, and pressed his hand against General Chandran's helmet. He struggled for a moment to reach Chandran's mind, then gave up and dropped his hand. "Nope. Can't do it. Can't feel you or control you at all. I guess that ends that argument."

Qadim glared at Kanvar and lifted his crossbow.

Kanvar squared his shoulders and looked Qadim in the eyes. "You have feared Nagas because of their power. But you need fear us no longer. Any man who fears losing his freedom can simply put on a helmet and walk away. Any Naga who attempts to take control of you will face armies of soldiers he can't control with weapons that can inflict wounds his dragon cannot heal. The balance of power has shifted. You need no longer kill every Naga that is born to keep yourself safe. All the Nagas who would try to enslave you are dead. Only those remain who have fought valiantly for your freedom."

"You have fought for us," General Chandran said, "as well as Tana, Rajan, and Denali here. No one can deny that Amar has worked tirelessly in our behalf. But what of the Naga guardsmen who enslaved so many thousands of people and forced them to build this city? Those men are our enemies."

"No, Khalid is the enemy," Kanvar said, motioning to the coffin. "He was our enemy, and he was theirs. I have seen into the minds of the guardsmen he intimidated, threatened, tortured and deprived of their free will. You cannot begin to understand the web of lies, deceit, and tyranny he spun over them. He brutally killed more of them than you can imagine. They, like you, have been struggling to free themselves. The ones who have survived and escaped Stonefountain will be haunted by his evil for the rest of their lives. The surviving Nagas of Navgarod are not your enemies."

Qadim's finger inched toward the trigger of his crossbow. "Kanvar is a Naga and a liar, and I say we kill him. The other Nagas will return, and if we want to survive, we better have an army waiting for them."

"You're going to kill the Great Blue Liberator while he's standing unarmed in front of you?" Kumar Raza said, raising his voice so all the humans gathered at the palace steps could hear. "You're going to murder him in cold blood?" Kumar Raza turned to the crowd and raised his spear. "What say you? Shall we kill the Great Blue Liberator? He's a Naga. Raise your voices if you want him dead. Kill the Great Blue Liberator!"

Silence descended on the crowd. No one spoke. No one cried out.

"I don't hear anyone cheering you," Kumar Raza said to Qadim. "Put your crossbow down, old friend. The war is over."

Qadim hesitated.

Kumar Raza reached out and eased the crossbow from his hands.

Kanvar let out a nervous breath.

It's a good thing that worked, Rajan muttered into Kanvar's mind. *My brother's an insane fool, but he knows how to play a crowd.*

Kanvar lifted his hand and spoke to the people gathered below him. "You are free. Stonefountain is yours. You can tear it to the ground as was done once before, or you can stay and live in the mansions you worked to build with your own hands. The Nagas make no claim to this palace, its throne, or this city. If you wish to leave it standing, may I suggest you elect leaders from each of the continents to govern here. Qadim for Varna, General Chandran for Maran, Bolivar for Darvat."

"And what of Kundiland?" General Chandran said.

Aadi stepped forward. "I will stay. Parvmer said there is a library here filled with the wisdom and wonder of old Stonefountain. I have been trained to read the ancient language. I'm not a Naga, so no human need fear me. I can bring ancient things to light that will make everyone's lives better."

Kanvar reached out and clasped Aadi's hand. "I can think of no better man for the job."

A cheer went up from the crowd which started chanting the names of the heroes that had freed them: Kumar Raza, Chandran, Bolivar, Qadim, and the Great Blue Liberator. The chant rolled back through the crowd out into the city.

An old human with gray hair and wrinkled hands pushed out of the mass of people and ascended the steps to Aadi's side.

"Giri?" Aadi said in surprise.

Giri held out his hand where a kitrat hatchling lay nestled. Aadi gasped and took the little dragon into his own hands, petting it and whispering to it softly.

"You can stay with me in my house," Giri said. "At least, I'm assuming I can claim it now that the Naga who lived there is gone."

Kanvar swallowed hard and rested his hand on the coffin. "Lord Taral is dead. It was his hand that wielded the blow that finished Khalid. He gave his life and his soul to free us all."

Dharanidhar let out a low rumble.

Kumar Raza frowned. "Khalid's spirit is in there. Are you sure?"

"Absolutely sure," Kanvar said. "But if someone were to open the coffin, Khalid could be freed. We must make sure that never happens."

I'll take care of that, Anilon said, putting a claw down on the coffin. *Give it to the Great Blue dragon pride. We will take it to Kundiland, bury it where no man can reach it, and guard it with our lives.*

Kanvar shared Anilon's suggestion with Kumar Raza and the other human leaders. After some discussion, they all agreed that would be for the best. With a roar and a spurt of blue fire, Anilon lifted the coffin from the ground and took to the air.

General Chandran crossed the space where the coffin had been sitting and grabbed Kanvar in a fatherly embrace.

"My boy, you did it. Kanvar, thank you. I feared you and I would never be able to be friends again."

"Oh, so we're friends now?" Kanvar said with a grin. "Does that mean I no longer have to polish your boots and clean out your chamber pot?"

"Well, I guess you've outgrown that. You're the Great Blue Liberator now, you and your dragon." Chandran stared up at Dharanidhar. "Of all the dragons to bond with, why him?"

"Dharanidhar likes to hunt," Kanvar said, reaching over his shoulder and fingering his crossbow, "And I'm a dragon hunter."

"So you are," Chandran said. "So you are."

Chapter Fifteen

Dharanidhar landed in Kanvar's chambers at the golden palace in Kundiland. He sank to the stone floor and quenched his thirst in the pool before setting Kanvar down. Their flight back from Stonefountain had been slow and easy. Naitik and the other blue dragons who carried Kumar Raza, Rajan, and Tana had stayed with them so the whole company arrived at the golden palace together. Kanvar had said goodbye to Raahi at Stonefountain but made plans to visit him soon when Raahi returned to Darvat. Denali and Frost decided to go home with Raahi's family to the cool heights of the Darvat mountains where Frost could grow strong.

Kanvar limped away from the pool to the human side of the chamber, which was laid out with all the luxuries of the palace. Dharanidhar curled up and watched Kanvar as he slid out of his armor and washed the grime of battle and travel from his face. Akshara's stone on Dharanidhar's chest winked blue in the sunlight.

"Father says Bensharie is bringing some medicine up to you from the village," Kanvar told Dharanidhar. "He'll be here soon."

Dharanidhar let out a rumble. Kanvar rubbed his aching legs and stretched. Bensharie and Amar flitted in through the window and landed. Dharanidhar accepted the medicine from them and drank the sour concoction without comment.

"Kanvar." Amar slid off Bensharie's back and strode over to Kanvar who greeted him with a welcome handclasp. "I'm glad you're back safely. I was worried when you stayed behind after the humans were free. They could have killed you."

Kanvar shrugged. "They didn't, though Grandfather tried to rile them into it."

"What, why?" Amar asked in dismay.

Dharanidhar filled the chamber with a deep laugh. *Because he is the Great Dragon Hunter, and he was trying to make a point.*

"What point could he possibly make by trying to kill you?"

"He had to prove to certain human leaders that the greatest majority of people understand now that not all Nagas are evil. The question had to be settled whether or not there would be peace between the remaining Nagas or more war. Qadim wanted the end of this rebellion to be like the last, with no Naga left alive, but the humans at Stonefountain decided that was no longer necessary. They felt confident in their ability to live freely along with the Nagas thanks to the iron helmets and weapons."

Dragonbound IX

The fact that we freed them from Khalid helped their decision as well, Dharanidhar said.

"So the humans want peace? I'm glad to hear it." Amar smoothed his golden robe and motioned for Kanvar to come with him. "Lord Theodoric and the Naga guardsmen are waiting in my . . . throne room. Did you know I had a throne room? I've never had to use it before."

"I've seen it in Tana's mind," Kanvar said. "It's where Parmver died."

Amar frowned and quickened his step down the hall. Kanvar let him go ahead. He couldn't hope to keep up; he was lucky to be on his feet at all though he knew the medicine would start working soon.

Tana met Kanvar in the hall outside the throne room. "How's Dhar?" she asked, taking Kanvar's hand.

"He'll be all right. I'm still standing, aren't I?" Kanvar kissed Tana on the cheek. "What are Theodoric and the guardsmen doing here? I told Devaj to send them to Navgarod."

"It seems they would not leave with the matter of the kingship unsettled. They're still torn between Amar and Devaj. You may have made peace between the Nagas and humans, but the Nagas are still at odds with each other."

Kanvar took a step toward the entrance to the throne room, but Tana held back. Thoughts of Parmver flitted through her mind.

"You can stay out here if you like," Kanvar said. "But I have to face these men. Are Rajan and Kumar Raza already there?"

"Yes, Raza went in with Theodoric right away," Tana said. "Rajan followed Amar in just now. I don't like the way these guardsmen think of me as if I'm some sort of inferior being for bonding with Vasanti. You go ahead. I'll come in when she gets here, and we'll see what they have to say about it when confronted by an angry Great Green dragon matriarch."

Kanvar chuckled. "I can't wait to see their faces." He limped into the room and found the Naga guardsmen who had survived the battle at Stonefountain gathered there. They stood at attention below the dais as Amar climbed the steps toward the throne with Rajan close beside to guard him. Devaj waited on the platform above, his face pale, his eyes sunken. Theodoric and Kumar Raza stood together at the bottom of the steps, facing the crowd, their hands on their sword hilts.

Maybe I should have left my armor on, Kanvar muttered to Dharanidhar as the crowd split and let him through. Unsettled mental whispers rang out against him. *Cripple, abomination, traitor, usurper, destroyer.*

Liberator! Kanvar shot back, drawing power from Akshara's dragonstone, which hung around Dharanidhar's neck. *You enslaved innocent humans, tore them from their homes, treated them shamefully. I don't care if you like me, but you should*

Dragonbound IX

know I will always fight for the freedom of this world. If any of you have a problem with that, let's finish it man-to-man right now.

Several guardsmen jerked their swords from their sheaths.

"No!" Devaj shouted. He raced down to his brother's side and drew his sword. "I will die before I let any of you touch my brother. He freed me from Khalid. He is a greater and nobler Naga than any of you can ever hope to be."

The guardsmen hesitated, their minds crossed with confusion. Hadn't it been His Majesty Devaj who had insisted from the beginning that Kanvar was the traitor who had murdered Amar to usurp the throne?

"Not so," Devaj said. "That was a lie. Khalid was controlling me, and he lied to you all. He arranged the circumstances to bring about my father's death so he could take me prisoner, body and soul. Kanvar is innocent of any wrongdoing. He is my deliverer, my liberator, and yours."

Shocked and embarrassed, the Naga guardsmen slid their swords back into their sheaths. Kanvar glared at them. "Fortunately, Khalid's plan to murder the king failed, thanks to an incredibly brave young lady." He turned to face the door, which slammed open, and Vasanti and Tana marched in.

A shout of alarm went up, and the guardsmen pressed back out of the way of Vasanti's tail that whipped behind her in anger. She bared her teeth at them, and her claws tore gouges in the golden floor as she stalked across the chamber to where Kanvar stood.

"This is Tana," Kanvar said, putting his arm around Tana's shoulders and hoping Vasanti wouldn't rub up against him. So stupid of him to take his armor off, thinking he was home safe. "It was her courage in the face of death, and her steely planning that saved King Amar's life."

Kanvar led Tana up the steps to where Amar stood with Rajan at his back to defend him. The two of them knelt before the king. "Your Majesty," Kanvar said. "We have served you faithfully and will ever remain in your service."

The hall went quiet. Kanvar wondered at the Naga guardsmen. So many continued to disbelieve Amar was their rightful king. What would it take to prove it to them?

Amar rested his hands, one on Kanvar's shoulder and one on Tana's. "My children, I cannot begin to thank you for your valiant service."

Kanvar felt Devaj climbing the stairs behind him. Kanvar rose and drew Tana aside as Devaj took their place, kneeling before King Amar. Devaj held the sword out to Amar in the flat of his hands. "My King, this is yours. Forgive me for all I've done, for all Khalid made me do. I wish no throne, no kingdom. Only let me serve you as I have ever done before he tore my free will away."

Tears glimmered in Amar's eyes as he lifted the sword from Devaj's hands. The runes on the blade flashed, and the pommel lit up with a golden glow. "Devaj, my son. Had you done anything that needed forgiving, I would forgive you. But you have not. All blame lies with Khalid.

We are blessed by the fountain this day that he is gone and we may return to our lives in peace." Amar lifted Devaj to his feet and embraced him. Then he motioned for Theodoric to come up.

Theodoric hurried forward, laid his sword at Amar's feet, and swore his oath, once again placing himself in Amar's service. Amar accepted his oath and turned his attention finally to the Naga guardsmen.

"Do you still question that I am your king? If so it is because your hearts burn within you in shame. You realize now that you have been in service to my enemy. It takes a strong man, and a humble one, to admit that he has been wrong. I am aware that many dark and cruel things happened at Stonefountain. Some of you participated willingly, and some out of fear. Today I pardon you all for past wrongs and invite you to pledge yourself to my service. No man will be forced to give me an oath, however. You are free men and may depart in peace if you wish only to serve yourselves. But know this, there are certain laws that I and those loyal to me will enforce with the sword if we must.

"First, you will not interfere with the humans on this side of the world or their governments.

"Second, you will not kill any infant, deformed or not. This is an abomination that I will not tolerate above all else.

"Third, any Naga, man or woman, may bond with any Great dragon of their choosing. The notion that Nagas can only bond with Great Gold dragons is false, and has been the cause of much suffering in this world. You see before you my son, Kanvar, who is bound to a Great Blue dragon; my wife's uncle who is bound to a Great Silver serpent; Tana, my dearest Tana, who is bound to this Great Green jungle matriarch; and this man—" Amar pointed to the base of the stairs where Karishi stood next to LaShawn, "—Lord Theodoric's grandson, is bound to a Great Metal dragon. You will accept them as your equals for they have fought bravely to return me to my rightful throne."

The Naga guardsmen muttered and shifted uneasily.

"Those are my laws," Amar continued. "I call on you now to give me your oaths, or go your way in peace. Lord Theodoric will retain his rule of Navgarod on the throne of Aesir. I intend to remain here with my family. Those who wish to serve me may do so here or in Aesir. I would not keep you from your homes and families. The time has come. Today you must choose to serve me or not."

LaShawn, with the aid of Karishi, was the first to mount the stairs and kneel at King Amar's feet, followed by Kumar Raza.

Kanvar held his breath. The Naga guardsmen seemed rooted in place, unwilling or unable to come forward. What had Khalid done to them? What compulsion had he put on their minds? Could Akshara's stone not free them?

They are free enough, Dharanidhar grumbled. *They are just stubborn men who have been caught in their wickedness and don't want to admit it.*

Dragonbound IX

You judge them too harshly, I think, Kanvar replied.

The crowd parted and Fistas came forward. Kanvar let himself smile. Fistas had covered his escape from Stonefountain with Aadi. Fistas mounted the steps but came first to Kanvar. His face was dark and troubled. "Where is my brother? Where is Taral?"

Kanvar's smile vanished. "Your brother is the noblest hero of us all. He gave his life and soul to stop Khalid. It was his hand that wielded the killing blow, a blow that took his own life as well. With his dying breath he told me to tell you not to grieve for him. He went willingly to stop Khalid. I am sorry. He is one of the greatest men I have ever met."

Fistas lifted a hand to Kanvar almost as if pleading. "Then, in the end, you saw his heart for what it really was? You saw the truth behind all of Khalid's perverse lies?"

"I saw the noble truth," Kanvar said. "And I promise you that is how the world will remember your brother. I will personally make sure that his true story will be written and told for the whole world to hear. Lord Taral was the best of men."

A small Great Gold dragon winged into the room and perched on the dragon throne next to Amar's throne. *I've already started writing an epic poem about him*, Bensharie said.

Fistas snapped his eyes up to look at the young dragon.

"Who is this?" a questioning mutter ran through the crowd.

The grin returned to Kanvar's face. He spoke so the whole room would hear. "This is Bensharie, the Great Gold

Dragon King, King Amar's dragon. He risked his life to take the king's bond as Rajahansa was dying. Yes, he's a little young, but he is perhaps wiser than us all."

Bensharie spread his wings and roared. *Give your oaths, silly Nagas, so we can be done with this tedious meeting and get to the feast my friends have prepared for you. We will have food and music and poetry. Come now, let us be brothers and friends.*

Bensharie's words, like a gentle gust of joy breath, seemed to wash away the ill-will and hesitation in the room. One-by-one the Naga guardsmen came forward and gave their oath of service to King Amar and reaffirmed their oaths to Lord Theodoric. Kanvar kept his arm around Tana throughout the proceedings. With each guardsman's oath, a little more tension seeped away from Kanvar's body, and his heart grew peaceful.

King Amar's countenance glowed with a tired grace as the Nagas united under his care. Devaj retreated to the edge of the room, his eyes veiled with sorrow.

He's hurting, Kanvar whispered to Dharanidhar.

Yes, Dharanidhar answered. *Devaj's spirit is wounded and may never quite heal, just like my legs. But he is alive and free. You have given him that much at least.*

Thank the fountain. Kanvar smiled at his brother. Devaj responded with a weak smile of his own.

When the last guardsman had given his oath, Bensharie lifted off from his throne and led the crowd to the waiting celebration. Hand-in-hand, Tana and Kanvar followed.

Epilogue

Dharanidhar perched on a rock ledge that jutted up from the jungle close to the shore. Hot sunlight glinted off the water, but could not penetrate the dense trees along the edge of the beach below him. He spread his great blue wings to the sky and let out a roar that echoed across the tops of the trees. On the sand in the shade of the trees, his mate crooned over the clutch of eggs as they rocked back and forth. Cool winds from the ocean kept the eggs from overheating in the hot climate.

Other dragons of the pride echoed their leader's jubilant call. Soon four new hatchlings would join their number.

Dharanidhar watched intently as an egg split open, and his first child pushed its head out into the world. It blinked wide eyes up at Dharanidhar and let out a squeak. Dharanidhar laughed. *That's right, little one*, he spoke into its newly awakened mind. *I'm your father. Welcome to the pride.*

Kanvar bent and rubbed the hatchling's head. Tana and Vasanti watched from the cover of the trees. Sunlight sparkled in Tana's eyes, and she smiled at Kanvar. *You see, Kanvar, I told you it was a good thing Dharanidhar took a mate to replace the one he lost long ago. A man is happier married than single.*

Kanvar grinned at her. *I know I will be.*

The little blue dragon clawed its way out of its shell and took a staggering first step. Its mother nudged it with her nose, and Kanvar moved out of the way to let her care for the hatchling.

"We should return to the village and give Dharanidhar and his family some privacy," Kanvar said, limping over to Tana. After the battle at Stonefountain, Dharanidhar had settled in his cave at the old nesting grounds near the Maran Colony so he could be closer to Kanvar. Dharanidhar's new mate and several of the younger dragons had joined him in starting a new pride. Tana and Kanvar had returned Mahanth's dragonstone to his burial mound and interred Indumauli's father's hide with the Great Gold dragons in the burial vault at the palace. Since then, the villagers had returned and the jungle village began to flourish once more.

Tana clasped Kanvar's hand as the two of them made their way to the Black River where a boat waited to take them home to the village. Every so often Kanvar glanced over at Tana, thinking about their coming marriage. Tana kissed him on the cheek. "Kanvar, Kanvar, don't be so impatient. We have the rest of our lives to live in peace and raise a family."

Kanvar grinned. "I just wonder what type of dragons our children will bond with?"

"You're getting a little ahead of yourself," Tana said, climbing into the boat.

Kanvar couldn't argue with that, but he couldn't help himself either. The world had become everything he'd ever hoped it would be, and he liked to imagine how his children would live in it.

About The Author

Rebecca Shelley (Rebecca Lyn Shelley) is the author of over 30 published books including the bestselling **Smart-boys Club** series as well as the popular **Red Dragon Codex** and **Brass Dragon Codex**. She loves writing about dragons and is excited to be writing the **Dragonbound** series. Her **Aos Si** *trilogy* will thrill fans of YA Paranormal Romance. To learn more or contact her, visit her website http://www.rebeccashelley.com.

If you have enjoyed reading **Dragonbound IX: Great Blue Liberator**, Rebecca would love to have you post a review on the site where you purchased it.

Worldshifters Preview

Hunted to the edge of chaos for crimes spawned by his untrained shifting powers, Alamon Truda hatches a desperate plan to turn the tables on his pursuers. His plan is threatened, however, when the son of the Goddess of Chaos steps into the human realm, shattering the world's balance. Now pursued by servants of both Order and Chaos, Alamon has to fight to keep both himself and the son of Chaos alive. The hunters chase him across the continent in a desperate bid to save the unraveling world, but both hunters and hunted stumble into the clutches of an unexpected foe.

Chapter One

Alamon Truda's sword hilt bit into his clenched hand. Sweat trickled down his neck and dropped into the dust that grimed everything in this mining town at the edge of the world.

He licked the salty moisture from his lips and glared at the jeering crowd that surrounded him in the street.

"Hand it over. Give it to her!" The angry miners' cries rose among the squat log cabins. The men's faces were set as hard as the stubborn rock they hammered deep underground for the hope of wealth that few obtained.

In his free hand, Alamon clutched a folded parchment, the claim to the gold mine he'd discovered in the Bitterstone Mountains that hemmed the town on three sides. He'd found the gold deposit because he *believed* it was there, and he'd promised himself it would be the last time he'd use his powers.

Calden, a burly miner with hunched shoulders and greed in his eyes, stepped out from the crowd. "Justice," he cried, raising his fist in the air. His other hand clenched his own sword, a heavy, crude blade that, wielded with a miner's strength, could be just as deadly as Alamon's sharp steel.

"This man raped my sister. I demand justice." Calden advanced another step.

His sister, Bliss, stood behind him at the edge of the bloodthirsty crowd, her stomach distended. Tears streaked her beautiful, heart-shaped face. Though Alamon had given his heart to her, the child she carried was some other man's, her accusations a lie to gain Alamon's gold.

Burning rage filled Alamon. Hot breath worked through his mouth. "I never touched her," he said through clenched teeth.

"The beam!" screamed the mob. "Let the beam settle this."

"The beam then," Alamon said. He was no stranger to it. A warning voice in his head urged him to hand over the claim and walk away. What was gold to him without Bliss?

But he was innocent.

So many other crimes hung over him—things he had truly done—that this accusation was one injustice too far.

Alamon strode down the street to the open space at the center of the mining town. He glanced at the drink house and longed for the taste of whisky to wash the dust from his mouth and the anger from his heart. It would have to wait.

The crude beam consisted of two pine trees stripped of branches, laid horizontally twice a man's height above the ground with the tips lashed together in the middle. Sharpened wooden stakes jutted up beneath it.

Alamon shoved the claim in his pocket, worked off his deer-hide jacket, dropped it at the beam's base, and climbed the stand to the top. The bark crunched beneath his boots as he stepped onto the trunk.

From this height, Alamon could see past the general store and the palisade that surrounded the town to where the human world ended. Beyond the edge of the world lay the Ellavion, the realm of Huius, Goddess of Chaos, where a lowland forest that had been in place for nearly half-an-hour *shifted* into a barren steppe with brown grass, rustling in a hot wind. After a moment, a granite mountain rose out of the steppe, and black clouds pelted its face with freezing rain.

The sun continued to burn over Alamon's head. Thankfully, the human world did not shift like the Ellavion. Alamon gazed into the face of Chaos and cursed the goddess he served. He'd almost settled down—would have married Bliss if she'd waited for him.

He imagined Huius's sultry voice laughing at him in response, a musical waterfall that rushed in his ears.

If things had been different, Alamon would have been living in the east, serving Illius, the God of Order, married to a wealthy woman his father had picked for him, admired and respected by everyone. But Chaos had swept him away in a torrent of power, and now he walked the beam for the only crime he hadn't committed.

Calden heaved himself up onto the beam opposite Alamon.

Alamon stepped out to meet him with a fatal air, one foot in front of the other, each step placed carefully between the knots and cracks in the wood.

He'd killed before. Hundreds of lives snuffed out in moments—innocent victims of his uncontrolled power. If

Dragonbound IX

Calden knew who Alamon really was, he'd be on the fastest horse he could find, riding the other way. But Alamon didn't want to use his powers here with so many people watching.

He'd hidden his identity, changed his looks, *believing* he looked like a different man. And he did, now. The hordes of hunters searching for Alamon Truda would not know him unless he *shifted* something here with all these witnesses.

If he *believed* Calden could not breathe, then Calden would not breathe. If he *believed* Calden's heart stopped beating then it would stop. But if Calden dropped dead without apparent cause, it would be a giant bell, tolling Alamon's position to every greedy soul who wanted the reward for his capture or death.

Alamon stood at the center of the beam with one foot on the tip of each sagging tree. He swung his sword in a lazy figure eight in front of him while he waited for Calden to inch out to meet him. Better to cut Calden down with the sword, or knock him from the beam and let him impale himself on the stakes.

Bliss's white face appeared at the edge of the crowd. She wrung her hands, seeing now that Alamon was more at home on the beam than her brother. Alamon forced her tear-streaked face and red lips from his mind and focused on Calden.

"Billy!" Bliss called to Alamon. "Billy, don't kill him. Don't hurt Calden. Please!"

Billy, the name he'd given himself when he'd come to this town, when he'd still hoped he could settle here like a normal man.

Calden wobbled, easing out toward Alamon with unsteady steps, his hands stretched to the side to center himself, but the heavy sword kept him off balance. The beam swayed and dipped farther the closer Calden got to Alamon. The tall stakes stood like an army of spears waiting to impale whatever victim gravity claimed. Alamon laughed at the thought of his own body splayed out on the stakes, a sharp wooden point thrust through his heart, protruding up out of his back. Death could be that easy if he chose to embrace it. A small part of him wished for it, but the rest clung to life with desperate vitality.

Calden swung at him in a wide arc that Alamon ducked. A simple thrust with his own blade while Calden fought to regain his balance would have ended it, but a flash of blue from the crowd caught Alamon's eye.

A young boy stared up at Alamon in horror. The wispy blond hair and cream-white face seemed familiar, but Alamon had never seen the lad before. The boy wore a blue tunic with a white rabbit on the front—the Kedra coat of arms. That, Alamon did recognize.

Kedra, like Truda, was a large householding out on the Midlan Plains. The Kedra Householding claimed neutrality, so Kedra men often served as armed escorts for merchant convoys that carried ore from the mines. The boy had probably come with his father, but Alamon didn't have time to search the crowd further.

He parried Calden's next thrust and twisted his sword, locking the blades together while he punched Calden in the face.

Calden staggered backward but remained standing.

The Kedra boy winced, too young to witness death like this, brutal and swift. Innocence glinted in his wide blue eyes.

Alamon swore. Calden deflected Alamon's blows, but he didn't have the grace it took to fight on the beam. While keeping Calden's sword busy, Alamon hitched his foot around Calden's ankles and kicked sideways, knocking Caldon's feet out from under him.

Calden fell.

The Kedra boy's wide eyes flashed through Alamon's mind. Alamon *believed* Calden would miss the stakes—for Bliss whom he'd loved, for the Kedra boy, and for his own innocence, lost years before.

Calden hit the ground wedged between two spikes against his chest, three more at his back, and one sticking up between his legs. He wiggled out from between them and stood unscathed.

Alamon flashed a smile at the Kedra boy, and his heart froze. A man in a matching blue tunic now stood beside him, a bow in his hand with an arrow already on the string, pointed at Alamon's heart.

Made in United States
Orlando, FL
26 February 2024

44154755R00117